Look for the Tor Double Action Westerns from these authors:

Max Brand

THE RED BANDANNA
CARCAJOU'S TRAIL

TOR

A TOM DOHERTY ASSOCIATES BOOK
NEW YORK

THE RED BANDANNA

Copyright 1933 by Street & Smith Publications, Inc. Copyright renewed © 1961 by Dorothy Faust. First appeared in *Western Story Magazine* as by "George Owen Baxter."

CARCAJOU'S TRAIL

Copyright 1932 by Street & Smith Publications, Inc. Copyright renewed © 1960 by Dorothy Faust. First appeared in *Western Story Magazine*.

A Tor Book
Published by Tom Doherty Associates, Inc.
49 West 24th Street
New York, N.Y. 10010

Cover art by Faba

ISBN: 0-812-51314-2

First edition: February 1991

Printed in the United States of America

0 9 8 7 6 5 4 3 2 1

THE RED
BANDANNA

CHAPTER 1
A Dead Man

THE COOK THREW HALF A DOZEN TOMATO CANS OUT OF the cook wagon, and the men began to knock them about with their Colts. Clancy Morgan, being a new hand on that ranch, took his turn with the rest, but he found that a quart can diminishes to too small a point when it has been hurled by a strong arm. He missed three times running. The other punchers looked at him and grinned, and nodded. Most of them were missing, too. Only the foreman and the freckled-faced kid from Arizona kept knocking holes in those cans.

That swarthy chunk of a cowpuncher, Bill, had taken no part in the proceedings, so Clancy Morgan went over and sat on his heels beside the taciturn man.

"You don't waste your time and lead on tin cans, eh?" asked Morgan.

"Yeah, and what's the use?" answered Bill. "New cartridges cost money. Maybe I could hit those tin cans as good as the next man. I dunno. I hate waste."

"Speaking of real shooting," said Clancy, "Danny Travis is the boy to shoot the spots out of everything."

Bill started. Or, at least, there seemed to be a movement of his entire body, but when Clancy Morgan looked down at him again, Bill was simply scratching one shin.

"Those new chaps of mine," explained Bill, "they got me all chafed up."

"You take new sheepskin, it sets that way," said Clancy.

He made his cigarette and looked across the sallow flats of the range, now blooming for a few moments in the sunset color. It had been a light day spent entirely in the saddle, with very little pulling and hauling. The cowpunchers were not sprawling on the ground, as usual in rest period; they were up and about, ready to play pranks. Their spirit was more like noon than night.

"Speaking of this gent—this Danny Travis," said Bill in a careful voice. "Just how good might he be?"

"An ace," said Clancy Morgan with youthful enthusiasm. "A regular ace." He broke off to remark: "Look at old Dick knock that can right out of the air! I'd like to be able to shoot like that." He shook his handsome young head. He was not over two and twenty, and his face was as happy as his heart, which had a way of singing all day long.

The shadows of life meant nothing to Clancy Morgan. They never had crossed him, and it seemed probable that they never *would* cross him. When he smiled, the flash of his eyes and the white glimmer of his teeth, and a bursting good humor and gentleness and kindly content with the world dissolved criticism. Men liked to have him around. So did women. If trouble ever came Clancy's way, one would expect it to be because women liked him too well.

"But I'm no good with a gun," continued Clancy Morgan. "I've spent my time learning to ride and rope and work cows; I've never had the spare hours to play around with a gun. But a gun can be useful, too."

"Yeah, a gun can be useful," said Bill, with a certainty that made his voice very quiet. "About this here Danny

Travis,'' he returned to the subject smoothly, ''might he be a friend of yours?''

''Why?'' asked Clancy Morgan cheerfully. ''Friend of mine? Why, I guess old Danny's about the best friend I have in the world. He taught me how to daub a rope on a cow. Good old Danny! He *is* a friend.''

''A friend is something worth having these days,'' said Bill profoundly. ''Yeah, or any day at all.''

''Danny tried to teach me to shoot,'' said Clancy.

Bill lifted his eyes slowly and sharpened them to look into the face of Morgan. ''He's a good hand, you say?'' muttered Bill.

''He's a *top* hand,'' declared Clancy. ''He's a top hand at everything. He can rope, and he can ride, and he can do about everything. He could be governor, or something like that, if he wanted to, I guess. The way he can talk, it's a caution! He's a *man*, is Danny Travis. You wouldn't think of him settling down, though, would you?''

''I'd as soon think of a hawk squatting down in a barnyard!'' exclaimed Bill.

''You know Danny, do you?'' asked Clancy.

''No, no,'' muttered Bill. ''I don't know him. I mean, the kind of a fellow you talk about, that can ride and rope and shoot and talk, and play a top hand at poker—that kind of a fellow, you'd expect him to keep on ranging and not to go and settle down on any patch of ground.''

''Did I speak about him being a good card player?'' asked Clancy thoughtfully.

''Sure you did,'' said Bill in haste. ''You spoke about him being a good shot and roper and rider and card player.''

Suspicion could not live in the mind of Clancy any longer than clouds can rule the sky in May.

''Cards are the way poor old Danny has always lost his money,'' said Clancy Morgan.

''Where would he have settled? Where would he have

5

taken up land?'' asked Bill. And he looked suddenly down to the ground and gripped a hand behind his back.

"Right down beside my home town," said Clancy Morgan. "Danny Travis sort of takes to me a little. I don't know why." He flushed with pride. "He says I'm a fool kid, but he sort of takes to me; and he settled on a piece of ground right outside of Tartartown. He's got a section that looks better for rabbits than for cows, but Danny'll be able to work it, all right. He always *is* able to do what he wants."

"Tartartown—that's south," murmured Bill.

He became silent. After a moment he rose and stretched. Then he walked off toward the place where the boss was pacing up and down. The back view of Bill was something like the back view of an ape, for the width of his shoulders, the length of his arms, and the shortness of his extremely bowed legs was accentuated. Clancy watched him walk up and down with the boss. They came to a halt and appeared to argue a point. Clancy was not interested in arguments.

He rolled down his blankets. It was not quite dark, and the moon would be up before very long; it was better to get to sleep before the moon slanted its pale light across the range. So Clancy rolled into the blankets, put his hands under his head, and fixed his mind on a pleasant thought, Olivia Gregor. Of late she was always his first thought. He never had asked her to marry him because it seemed an impertinence to speak of marriage before he was further on his way toward an established home; but he always thought of her with a sense of possession. Certain moments of silence had passed between them that made him feel sure. Now he closed his eyes. He thought of her as he'd last seen her when she pulled up her horse, and her hand and her laughter went out to him. He had wanted to pick her off that little mustang and hold her high in his arms. She had known what he wanted, too. Girls always know. They're clever that way.

So Clancy Morgan smiled, and pleasant sleep was clouding his brain when he heard the voice of the boss talking to the foreman.

"I told him I counted on him to finish the job. He wouldn't stay. There was something working in him. He saddled up and took the south trail."

Some of the sleep rolled back from the mind of Clancy Morgan. The south trail led toward Tartartown, and in Tartartown lived Olivia Gregor.

"It's too bad," said the foreman. They kept their voices lowered as they made down their blankets for the night. "It's too dog-gone bad, because Bill's a good cowhand. And he handled that string of outlaws that I gave him like they was house pets. There's something to that Bill."

"I'll give you an idea what," said the boss.

"All right. What's so mysterious?"

"I looked him in the eye while I was talking to him," said the boss. "You know how a resemblance misses you for a long time and then comes back sudden?"

"Yeah. I know."

"I'd been lookin' at Bill for days. All at once, tonight, it hit me between the eyes—it's nobody but Jasper Orping."

The name awakened Clancy Morgan and brought him up to one elbow, blinking. There was only one Jasper Orping. The ghosts of his dead men would agree to that. Moreover, on a day, had there not been bad blood between Danny Travis and Jasper Orping? It was a thing that increased the air of dignity which surrounded Danny Travis—that he could have fallen out with Jasper Orping and have remained intact in life and limb.

"That ain't Jasper Orping," declared the foreman. "Jasper's three inches taller, and his legs are straight, pretty near. I seen him once. I only had a rear view, but I seen him once.''

''Sure, it ain't Jasper. I ain't said it was Jasper. I said it reminded me of Jasper, is all. It ain't Jasper. It's Jasper's brother, Bill.''

Clancy Morgan sat up straight. Suspicion was something he detested and shut out from his mind as a rule, but this was more than suspicion. It was a straight trail to trouble. Clancy Morgan disbelieved in tales of murderers, traitors, gunmen, and crooks and scoundrels in general. He never had seen a killing. He never expected to see one. When he heard of acts of villainy, he always made a mental reservation. What we have not seen remains a fairy tale.

But this was different. Bill had been singularly interested in the name of Danny Travis. He had brought up the name again and again. The moment he knew where Danny was to be found he had gone to the boss, drawn his pay, and hit the south trail—toward the place where Travis lived! Did Bill mean well? Only a child or a fool could think that he did. He must warn Danny.

Clancy Morgan turned out of his blankets, dressed with a few swift motions, and stood up as a great rim of red gold pushed above the eastern horizon. At least, he would have moonlight to show his way through the hills.

The boss was just pulling off his boots when Morgan stood before him, saying:

''I've got to ride to Tartartown. I've remembered something. I've got to go!''

The boss slammed onto the ground the boot he had just drawn off.

''You aim to go and come back?''

''Yes,'' said Clancy.

''If you go, you stay.''

''All right,'' said Clancy. ''I'm sorry.''

''Running out on the middle of the job—like a lot of

pikers—like a lot of tinhorn sports!" exclaimed the boss. "What's the matter with you, kid? What's on your brain? What's biting you? That's what I'd like to know."

"It's something terribly important. I can't tell you."

"Well, get out, then, and hurry back as soon as you can!"

Clancy Morgan turned.

"This got anything to do with Bill leaving?" asked the boss curiously.

It was not the custom of Clancy Morgan to leave questions unanswered. This time he felt he should turn and tell a lie, but lies did not come smoothly off his tongue, so he simply walked straight on as though he had not heard.

He found his horse and got the hobbles off it and the saddle on its back. It was a four-year-old, not quite hardened, but with promise of making a cutting horse one day. Clancy Morgan regarded it sometimes with impatience, but usually with awe. What did children of four know, compared with the knowledge possessed by this mustang?

He bade no farewells, but took the road south on the long trail. Ordinarily he would have made that ride in two stages, but this time he dared not pause. If one of the Orping crew wanted the scalp of Danny Travis, he must rush the warning through.

He saw the moon climb up to the lonely center of the sky. He saw it slope westward, whitening the hills. The dawn came, and a great weariness ached behind his eyes. The mustang began to stumble. He eased the horse of its burden and walked several miles. With sunup he was in the saddle again, and rode through the gap of the north trail into view of Tartartown. All the houses blinked their windows at him, like signal lights, and a sudden warmth of assurance and relief came over him, for this was home.

Tartartown was hardly more than a sprinkling of houses gathered around the crossing of two rather dim trails. From the little cluster of buildings at the crossing, the outskirts grew more and more sparse until the ranches began, mere spots that the unpracticed eye could hardly find without much searching. For it was not a land of trees; neither was there a big growth of shrubbery. It was a land of cactus and bitter mesquite.

But scenery makes no more than a backdrop, and it is people who must fill the stage. Clancy Morgan no longer had a house, but still Tartartown was home when he thought of all the faces and all the voices that he could call into his eye and into his ear. His heart swelled as he thought of the goodfellowship of the men and the gentleness of the women. Suddenly he was assured that no real danger could have been moving toward Danny Travis. He felt he had been a fool to make this long ride for nothing. But being here, of course, he would go to see Danny.

He headed down through the town. It was quite early, but not too early to find a Western town awake. He saw Dick Richards entering his blacksmith shop.

"I'm in a hurry, Dick. Seeing you later!" he called.

"Hey, Molly—hey, Dickie—Clancy's come back to town!" thundered the blacksmith. And he stepped out into the street to follow Morgan with his eyes.

A sweet pang of joy slid up the spine of Morgan and rose like a summer sun in his mind. This was home!

Doctor Walters came out on his veranda.

"My dear boy! My dear Clancy!" he cried.

"I'm coming back, doctor," said Clancy. "I'm in a hurry, but I'm coming back!"

"Martha," called the doctor, "here's Clancy Morgan, looking as brown as a berry."

"Berries are not brown, silly," said the sharp voice of Mrs. Walters from inside the house.

And Clancy Morgan laughed. What a good world!

Little Harry Stephens rushed at him barefooted, barelegged, out of the vacant lot beside his father's house.

"Hey there, Clancy—Clancy!" he yelled, incredulous, squeaking with joy.

"I'm coming back," said Clancy Morgan.

"I'll tell Nell," said the boy. "She'll just yell! Hey, Clancy, I'm glad!"

Clancy Morgan went on. He wished he might be passing the house of the Gregor family, but that, unfortunately, was not his luck. And it was right to save the best for the last. When he saw Olivia—

The houses cleared away. Before him appeared the twisting, dim trail which led in the direction of Danny Travis's new house. It was just over the hill—and there was Danny himself coming out of the mesquite. He saw the rider. Something flashed out of the hand of Travis as he hurried forward, waving.

In front of the little 'dobe house they met. Danny Travis looked flushed, perhaps from walking through the soft, deep sand among the mesquite. But Clancy Morgan paid little heed to this as he hurled himself off his horse and gripped the hand of his friend.

"It's like years and years, Danny!" shouted Clancy Morgan.

The older man looked him up and down, almost coldly. Then he nodded.

"More shoulders and less stomach on you than there used to be, Clancy," said he.

"Oh, they work you up there!" said Morgan. "Is there some barley in that shed? This pony has come a ways."

"Yes, he's gaunted up a bit," said Travis. He turned his solemn face toward the shed that leaned against one end of the cabin. "There's no grain in there. I'll tell you the best idea—I'll go back into town with you. We'll have a feed ourselves, and we'll feed the horse, too. Come along, Clancy."

"Before I've seen how you've fixed up the place?" exclaimed Morgan, stepping to the door.

11

"Get out of that!" commanded Dan Travis.

His voice had a metal clang in it that flicked through the blood of Morgan like cold air. But the hand of Clancy already had struck the door, knocking it open with a stagger, and inside, a pale thing among the shadows on the floor, he saw the face of Bill Orping. He saw the body of Bill Orping stretched out. And he knew that the man was dead!

CHAPTER 2
The Curious Dog

THE DOOR SWUNG BACK WITH A SLAM. IT WAS A LOUDER noise, at that moment, than the explosion of a bomb. Clancy turned. Travis, knees flexed a little, seemed ready to leap at him, and the hand of Travis was moving as though it had just put away a gun in the holster lashed to his right thigh.

Part of the quality in Travis that intrigued Clancy Morgan was this savagery which was always as close to his skin as the claws of a cat are to the velvet of its paw. It showed more often in some flash of the eyes, some hardening of the voice. But now it had come to a matter of actual threat. That gun, beyond a doubt, had been in his hand!

It was almost a greater shock to Clancy Morgan than the sight of the dead man inside the cabin. But there are such things as involuntary reactions, Morgan knew.

He moistened his white lips.

"Well?" said Travis, without parting his teeth.

"Danny—I—He's dead," whispered Morgan.

"You had to be a fool and butt in," said Travis. "You

13

had to play the young fool. The next time you come to a man's house—'' He stopped.

"You don't mean that, Danny!"

Travis stared at him.

"I'm going inside."

"Yeah. You'd wanta do that, too," said Travis.

Morgan put his hand on the door. There was no further objection. Travis pushed past him and stood in the center of the room, looking down at the dead man. Morgan followed.

He had wanted to see the improvements in the house; now he looked at these first. There was an open hearth with a crane from which pots hung; Travis always had liked Mexican ways of doing things. There was a good table, homemade and stronger than any store product; Travis was an excellent mechanic. There was a bunk covered with a goatskin; another goatskin lay on the earthen floor of the hut beside the bunk. In one corner was a shelf of books. The tinware on the pantry shelves shone as though a woman kept house here. That was like Travis, too. He was complete in all ways; he was a law and a sufficiency unto himself. He had even carved some decorative designs on the under faces of the cross beams; and he had colored those designs with bright red and blue and yellow, Mexican style.

After seeing these things, Clancy Morgan was able to look down at the dead man without feeling faint.

Bill Orping had been shot straight through the heart. The red patch was right over it; and there was an aperture in the middle of the stain. It was a big, round hole. It hardly looked as though a revolver bullet had made that hole; it was rather as though a charge of buckshot had been fired at close range.

Clancy Morgan lost his breath and sat down in one of the comfortable homemade chairs—Travis was always working away with wood; his hands could never be idle; he was like a sailor.

Bill had been a good cowhand. He could handle a rope in a high wind as though the hemp were heavy, liquid-flowing rawhide. Bill was a good man with a branding iron, too. He never burned the calves too deep. He was good on a fence line, too. He was good all around, except when it came to spinning yarns of an evening. And now he lay there, finished.

His eyes, open a mere crack, seemed to mock Clancy, seemed to be spying on him.

"He's dead," said Clancy.

He heard a faint rustling sound. Travis was making a cigarette, licking it to glue the paper fast, turning down one end of it, lighting it. The match snapped far away out of the fingertips of Travis.

"Yeah. He looks kind of dead," said Travis calmly.

"I recollect—" began Clancy.

"What?"

"Nothing," said Clancy. He'd been about to tell how he saw Bill get covered with mud one day, tailing a steer out of a waterhole, where it had bogged down. He was ashamed that he had wanted to tell this thing in a casual manner. He was ashamed because his first sight of death had not driven through his brain like a bullet. It seemed perfectly natural. It was hardly more than looking at a dead deer.

"The Culversons come down this way every day about this time," said Travis. "They mostly stop in here."

"What'll we do?" said Clancy, coming to his feet.

"I don't know."

"What did you—how did it happen—I mean, did you shoot him with a shotgun?"

"No," said Travis, and touched the holster at his side.

"But that's not a half-inch wound!" exclaimed Clancy.

Travis merely stared at him. Then Clancy remembered. A

.45-caliber does not make a great wound where it enters, but it is apt to mushroom somewhat and make a frightful place where it comes out through the body.

"Danny, you didn't happen—you didn't shoot him in the back?" he gasped.

"Well?" said Travis.

He looked straight at Clancy and set his jaw. He said nothing.

That was like Travis. He was not one to explain. If you doubted him, you doubted him. That was all. A man is a friend or he's not a friend. There's nothing else to it.

"Danny," said Clancy, "it's not that I think anything wrong. I know you only did what you had to do. I know everything was all right, only—"

"He was a fool," said Travis.

He made a gesture with his foot toward the dead body.

"If his brother finds it out! If Jasper Orping finds out—then what?" breathed Clancy.

"Oh, I'll take care of Jasper Orping, and I'll take care of any other man," said Travis calmly. "Only—it's rotten, that's all. This fool—he came down and crowded me. What are his brother's arguments to him? He came and crowded me. I didn't want to hurt the fool. He was nothing to me. I tried to let him off easy. But he crowded me. He made me pull a gun. That's all. He won't crowd anybody else!"

It seemed vaguely strange to Clancy that a man can be shot through the back while he is crowding an enemy. But it never occurred to Clancy to doubt Travis. It would have been easier to doubt himself; and much easier, at that.

"What'll we do?" asked Clancy. "If people see him like this. Shot from behind, I mean."

He picked up a gun that lay on the floor and broke it open. One cartridge had been fired from it.

"He took a crack at you, all right, Danny?" he asked.

"Well, there's a bullet been fired from that gun, hasn't

16

there? And that's Bill Opring's gun, isn't it?'' demanded Travis.

"When they see the wound is in his back—'' said Clancy.

"That's the rotten part," declared Travis. "People don't realize even a fellow like Bill Orping can lose his nerve the last minute and try to run for it.''

"And you couldn't hold up?''

"Don't talk like a fool! I was shooting when he swung around. Ask people to believe what I say. That's all. Just ask 'em. A lot of fools, is what I say. And a lot of 'em would like to get my scalp!''

His face went dark and savage, and he made another gesture with his foot toward the dead man. "I thought I was through with all this kind of stuff," said Travis.

"If the Culversons are coming," said Clancy, "we've gotta do something. We've gotta do something quick. What?''

"I don't know," said Travis. He seemed strangely helpless.

"We've got to get him out of here. That's the first thing.''

"Maybe you're right. Take his legs. I'll take him by the shoulders.''

Clancy stooped and picked up the legs of the dead man close to the knees. They were as heavy as lead; they slid out of his grasp like quicksilver.

"Wait a minute," he said.

He took off his bandanna and knotted it closely around the knees of Bill Orping. That gave him a good handhold. He walked first through the door.

"Over there to the right, in that patch of mesquite," directed Travis.

So Clancy walked on. The feet of Bill Orping kept bobbing rapidly up and down; the sun flashed on the toes of the boots. They entered the mesquite tangle. Clancy

17

looked around before he lowered his burden, and saw how Travis held the dead man by the shoulders, and how the head of Orping was hanging down. It made him sick. Dead fish hang like that, loose and limp, from the line of the fisherman. He put down the body, unknotted the bandanna from the knees of Orping, and arose.

"What were you doing over there in that other mesquite tangle when I first saw you?" asked Clancy, with no thought in his mind except how the sun was beating fiercely down into a dead face.

"I was digging some mesquite roots. I was out of wood," said Travis.

"Great Scott," muttered Clancy, amazed and awed. "You left him dead in your cabin, and you went out and dug mesquite?"

"I was bothered," said Travis. "I wanted to do something and clear my brain. I wanted to give my head a chance to work."

That was just like Travis. He always had to have his hands employed.

"What about the horse Orping rode?" said Clancy.

"It's in back of the house."

"We ought to do something about it."

"We'll peel the saddle off of it. We'll turn it loose," said Travis.

That seemed an incomplete solution to Clancy.

"We ought to bury Orping now," he suggested.

"We haven't got time," said Travis. "The Culversons are coming along pretty quick. We haven't got time!"

He dropped the gun of Orping on the ground close beside the body. Then he hurried to the back of the house, appeared again riding Orping's mustang, and took it up the trail. When he came opposite the mesquite tangle he dismounted, cut the horse across the flank with his quirt, and sent it flying. It disappeared quickly among the low hills.

Then the two went back to the house together.

"Tell me!" said Clancy. "Something has to be done!"

"There's blood on the floor. We'll clean it up first," said Travis.

He was perfectly calm. He was so calm that the heart of Clancy stopped racing so fast.

When they got into the cabin again they examined the spot where the body had lain. The earth was dark; the blood showed hardly at all. Travis simply kicked away some of the surface soil and let it scatter. Then he brought in fresh earth from outside and stamped it down on the spot.

He stood back and examined the place. He looked around him deliberately, as though to spot anything that might bear witness against him.

"After the old Culversons go by," said Travis, "we can catch up Orping's horse and load Orping on it, and take it down to the river. That's only five miles. The river will cover him, and cover his horse, too. Orping will just be something that rode off the face of the earth. That's all."

"We'll have to wait till dark to carry him down there," said Clancy. "Somebody would see us. There's always kids fishing in the river."

"Well, we'll wait till dark, then."

Clancy closed his eyes and groaned. "Suppose somebody should find the body during the day?" he asked.

"If the pinch comes, I simply say that a couple of men went by not long after sunup. I heard a couple of shots. That's all I know. I thought somebody was shooting at rabbits. It didn't bother me. I was cooking breakfast and I didn't even go outside. I thought it was rabbits."

He smiled a little.

"You see how it is, Clancy. There's always a way out!"

"I see," said Morgan vaguely.

He started to make a cigarette.

"You need a good swig of coffee," said Travis, moving toward the fireplace. Blue wood smoke from the dying fire moved about his shoulders.

"Wait a minute!" exclaimed Clancy, springing up.

He stood with his hand at his throat.

"Well?" asked the quiet voice of Travis.

"Where's my bandanna? I had a bandanna on! Did I leave it out there somewhere in the mesquite tangle?"

"Must be around the cabin somewhere. I saw you untie it from Orping's knees."

"Where is it, then? Help me look. No, Danny, it must have brushed out of my hand! I'll go back and get it!"

"Go ahead. I'll have the coffee ready when you come back."

Clancy stepped to the door, opened it, and passed out. But down the trail he saw a buckboard coming, drawn by two little down-headed mustangs, and with the dumpy figures of a man and woman in the driver's seat. A small mongrel dog ran under the heads of the ponies, jumping up at them now and then. Its sharp voice came across the air to the ears of Clancy.

He moved hastily back into the cabin.

"Somebody's coming. I can't go out there now."

"Who's coming?"

"Man and woman in a buckboard. And a dog. Two horses."

"That's nothing but the Culversons. They're blind in one eye and can't see out of the other. You know the Culversons."

"No. They're new people. I don't know 'em. Danny, I've got to have that bandanna!"

Travis poured out a tin cup of coffee.

"Why?" he asked. "Cold in the neck—or cold in the feet?"

He even laughed.

"Take one of mine, brother, and then you'll be all dressed up again."

He went to a small box like a sailor's chest, opened the lid of it, and took out a blue silk bandanna, polka-dotted with small rounds of white.

"Put that on, Clan," said he.

Morgan hesitated.

"Mine was red and yellow," he objected.

"Come on! Come on!" urged Travis. "Don't get the panics. What's the matter with you?"

"I'm sorry," muttered Clancy Morgan, and knotted the bandanna quickly around his throat.

The barking of the dog, the pounding of hoofs, the rattling of wheels, the grinding of iron tires in the sand drew close and paused in front of the cabin.

"There they are," said Travis. "They're a pair of old dummies. They won't see anything. They'll sing out and ask if I want anything in town—anything heavy they can bring in the buckboard. They're a good-hearted pair of old plugs!"

A footfall came to the door, which was pushed open by a bent, smiling old man with a tuft of white beard on his chin. His lips pursed a little over a toothless mouth. He made a smacking sound when he talked.

"Hullo, Danny," said old Culverson. "Look at here what I found. Never seen such a coin in my days!"

Travis went to the door and took it. He bent over it.

"That's just an old Spanish coin, Pop," said he. "That's all it is."

"That all? There ain't no value attached to it?"

"No, not much!"

The little black-and-tan mongrel pushed through the door and went sniffing about the cabin.

"Well," said old Culverson, "I kind of like it. I might polish it up and use it for a watch charm, eh?"

21

Clancy did not hear the answer. He was watching the dog fall to work with furious energy, scratching at the place where the blood of Orping had soaked into the floor!

CHAPTER 3
Suspected

"Howdy, Danny!" called the shrill voice of the woman, who still sat in the buckboard. "Anything hefty you want us to fetch out from town?"

"Nope. Not a thing, thanks," said Travis.

"Here, Jingo! Here, Jingo, you little fool! He's tearin' the nation out of your floor, Danny," said Mr. Culverson.

"Oh, that's all right, Pop," said Travis. "He thinks he smells a rat, maybe."

"Maybe. He's a fool, worthless thing, but he's kind of got used to us, and we've got used to him. Here, Jing, drat you!" He broke off, to add: "Hello, you got a friend with you, Danny?"

"Come here, Clancy," said Travis. "It's Clancy Morgan. This is Pop Culverson."

The half-cold hand of the old man gripped that of Morgan.

"So you're Clancy Morgan, are you?" said Culverson. "And I've heard aplenty about you, son, around this town. And all good, too. All mighty good, boy! I'm glad to see you. I'm right glad to see you. If you step by our way, remember that the latch hangs on the outside. I wanta set and yarn with you about your dad sometime. I used to know your dad. I knew him up in Nevada, and a right fine man Joe Morgan was. And a right fine son he's left behind him, I can see with half an eye. Hi, Jingo! You little fool, you tryin' to trip me up?''

For the dog had darted through the doorway, and now went scuttering through the sand toward the mesquite patch in which lay the body of Bill Orping.

The three men now stood in front of the house as old Culverson went back toward the buckboard, saying: ''Here's young Clancy Morgan, whose pa I used to know right well.''

Morgan went to the rig and shook hands with the little, fat, smiling woman. She kept bobbing her head at him.

''I knew Joe Morgan, too,'' said she. ''He was a man a girl could never forget.''

''Now, now,'' said her husband.

''Look,'' said Mrs. Culverson. ''He takes after Danny Travis and wears blue-and-white bandannas—and that's a thing one don't see much on this part of the range.''

''It is,'' agreed Culverson, ''but I—''

A mournful wailing came from the mesquite.

''Here, Jingo!'' called Culverson. ''What's that fool dog gone and found? Here, Jingo, Jingo! I never seen a dog to waste more time. Here Jingo!''

''Go get him,'' commanded Mrs. Culverson. ''You know how he is. You know he won't scarcely ever come when he gets all excited. My heart, sounds like he's found a dead horse, or something!''

Old Culverson was already on his way. Clancy Morgan, stirring uneasily, looked at Travis, but Travis appeared to have noticed nothing. He was resting a foot on the hub of the nearest axle and talking cheerfully as Culverson disappeared into the brush.

"Hi! Hi!" shouted Culverson. "There's somebody—there's something—there's—"

His voice choked.

"There's something wrong," said Travis to Mrs. Culverson. "Come on, Clancy!"

And as they started, he added under his breath: "Run right where we walked when we carried the body out. Run right behind me, Clancy!"

So Clancy Morgan ran at the heels of Travis from the 'dobe hut into the mesquite, where they found Pop Culverson on his knees beside the body, as though he would not be convinced by a mere glance that he had found one of his fellow mortals dead.

He looked up at the pair of them with a gray face and a shaking head.

"Great Scott! Right outside my house!" Travis exclaimed.

Clancy Morgan said nothing. He was seeing the dead man with new eyes, to which the fear of the law lent a stronger vision.

"How come this, Danny?" said Culverson, laboring to his feet.

He waved his hand, and Jingo no longer sniffed at the dead body, but sprang away to a distance. Into the mind of Clancy Morgan sprang something about: "And the beasts of the field and the birds of the air shall consume them!"

"I wish I knew how come," said Travis. "Yes, sir, that's what I wish! Right outside my house! Is he long dead?" he went on, leaning over the body. "No sir, not long enough dead to be cold. By the jumping thunder, Pop, I know who it was!"

"Who, Danny, who?" asked Culverson eagerly.

"A pair of men rode by the house while I was cooking my breakfast. I heard a couple of shots that sounded right in my ears. Sounded like rifle shots. I thought they were shooting at rabbits or something. I didn't even step outside to look. You know how you feel sort of dead and lazy before breakfast?''

"I know," agreed Culverson. "but no rifle ever tore that hole. And there's a revolver lyin'—"

"So it is," said Danny Travis. "But it sounded like rifles."

He reached toward the gun.

"Don't touch that gun! Don't touch it!" warned Culverson. "Somebody who knows more law than either of us three had oughta see just how he's laid out before he's touched. A lot hangs by that, I've heard and read."

"You're right," agreed Travis. "A lot might hang by that. We'd better stand away. The footprints might mean something."

"They might," said Culverson. "And you heard the shots? Well, a revolver will sound like a rifle sometimes. It depends upon the air, sort of. And then, you were inside the house. Maybe this that I picked up will mean something."

And he held up the yellow-dotted red bandanna of Clancy Morgan. It seemed to Morgan as if it was the lifting of a hostile flag, as if there were treason in that small bit of silk. He could feel fear freezing his face and making his eyes bulge.

"Yeah, that may have some meaning, so let's see it," said Danny Travis.

"Don't be askin' to see it till I've showed it to them who might know," muttered Culverson. "This county is a sight too big. This here happens—and the sheriff is clean over in Tuscamora! How long will it be before there's even somebody who knows who he is?"

The heel of Travis descended on the foot of Clancy Morgan. Then Clancy realized. Of course, he would have to speak up; he had ridden on the same ranch with this man.

"Why," he said, "the fact is I know him, all right. I've been riding with him on the Gresham place for quite a while. I'm still riding there!"

"Not exactly," said Culverson, rather dryly. "Looks to me like you're riding down here in Tartartown. But what might his name be?"

"Bill was all I ever heard him called," said Clancy Morgan. Then he added reluctantly: "But I've heard the boss say he looked a whole lot like one of the Orping men."

Culverson started.

"Orping? And by thunder, he *does* look like Jas Orping himself. Only smaller. This is a bad business. If this here is Bill Orping, Jas will make trouble, and he's one knows *how* to make trouble!"

He shook his head. The voice of his wife called with shrill inquiry from far away.

"We'd better pick up the body and put it in the back of your rig, Pop," suggested Travis. "There's nobody that represents the law in our town. You're as good a head as any to look around. It's no business leaving the body out here to the sun and the flies."

"You're right, Danny," answered Culverson. "I guess I've seen all I'm likely to see. Here's where his horse come in from the road. Here's where he fell out of the saddle. There's where the horse ran off. Will you fellows try to catch that scary hoss? Because maybe there'll be some sort of evidence in it. Shot in the back! It kind of makes me sick. I've seen dead men, Danny. But Heaven pity the poor soul who gets shot through the back! He didn't have no chance."

"He must have been riding up the trail with somebody," argued Travis. "He turned off the trail into the mesquite right here. His friend that was with him pulls a gun and shoots him in the back. As he falls, being a fighting man, he manages to get out his gun and fire—once. I suppose he just dented the sky, and that was all. We'd better get the body over to your rig. We'll carry him. You go and tell your wife to sit there and face forward. You quiet her down!''

Culverson went off with a step that waddled slowly through the deep sand. Travis said quietly:

''This is the best chance we could have. This gets the body away from the place before somebody with a hawk eye spots the thing. Pick up his legs, Clan.''

''I hate to touch him. I can hardly make myself touch him,'' breathed Clancy Morgan.

''Sure you do. So do I. But we've got to. Grit your teeth and dig in.''

They carried the body slowly to the wagon and slid it into the back of the buckboard. Travis brought some old sacking and covered it from head to toe; Culverson and his wife were talking rapidly in horrified voices.

''You catch that runaway horse. I'll go in with them,'' said Travis to Clancy Morgan. ''I heard the shots. I'll have to be giving testimony or something, I suppose.''

So Morgan watched the buckboard pull away while he himself mounted his weary horse and rode down the trail of Orping's mustang. A good two miles he was obliged to travel before he found the mustang, and then there was a further half hour before he could catch the brute. Finally he toiled back to the trail, and so along it toward the town, with the weary mustang of the dead man pulling firmly back on the lead rope.

He'd passed the house of Travis when, over the hill from town, came Travis himself, his horse at a lope. He waved a hand to arrest the course of Clancy Morgan, and then pulled up beside him.

''Hell's popping,'' said Travis. ''Drop that rope. Let the mustang go. And hike out of here. Bury yourself in the hills, Clan. Fade out till things quiet down. I'll let you know when everything's blown over."

Clancy Morgan stared at him, squinting his eyes. The sun was very strong. He felt the burn of it on his chin as he put back his head a little. "What's the matter?"

"That bandanna. Everybody and his brother and sister saw you come through town wearing a red bandanna like the one that was picked up by the body of poor Orping. And Culverson saw you in a blue-and-white one, like mine. People are talking to beat the band. Everybody's having a say. Skin out, brother. Skin out."

The world expanded to a bleak immensity, through which Clancy saw a small form pursued by throngs. That small figure was himself.

"Wait a minute, Danny. You mean they're hanging this job on me?"

"Don't argue. Ride!" commanded Dan Travis. His harsh face darkened still more, and he waved a peremptory arm. "I know what's for your own good, boy. Get out of here, and get fast. Ride over toward Allerton. I'll come and pick you up and give you the news in a day or two."

"Dan, you mean they're after me? They accuse me of murder, when—"

"When I did it?" answered Travis. "That's what I mean. I'm warning you now. Skin out. I did the job, and you're blamed for it. I could explain the thing till the cows come home, and they'd simply say it was friendship that makes me talk. They know I'm not the sort to let a bunky down. Clancy, get out, and get fast!"

The heart of Clancy Morgan shrank smaller than the head of a pin. Once a man began to run, the fear grew vaster behind him. He knew that. You don't fear the nightmare in the dark until you turn your back on it.

He freshened his grip on the lead rope of Orping's horse.

"No," he said slowly. "I'll ride on into town."

"You fool!" shouted Travis, losing his patience. "If you go into town, I'll have to break my neck to get you out of trouble. Show some sense, Clan!"

He lowered his voice suddenly to an appeal.

"You see how it is," he added. "A man shot in the back. That's murder, in this part of the world, no matter what the evidence may be otherwise. The bullet hole talks for itself. If you go to town they're apt to lynch you."

Clancy Morgan drew in his breath. He wanted to run. Every nerve in his body trembled. But if he ran, he gave up all his past life. All he had been became a dead thing. And among the dead things would be Olivia Gregor.

"I'm going to town," he said, and spurred his mustang into a trot.

"Well, you poor—" began Travis.

But he stopped his words. He did not follow. Clancy Morgan went into Tartartown alone.

CHAPTER 4
Lynching Party

THE LITTLE TOWN SEEMED DESERTED. THERE WAS NOT A face nor a voice until he came close to the hotel and saw the whole of Tartartown gathered there like iron filings on paper above a magnet. People stood about in groups with serious faces, making their expressions very solemn; he knew that in their hearts they were enjoying something worth talking about. And inside the hotel, in one of the lower rooms, would be the body of poor Orping.

Travis had called him that. Even Travis, who did the shooting, had just now spoken of "poor Orping."

Clancy was bewildered by the actions of Travis. Not that he had the slightest fear Travis would let him stay in serious trouble on account of something Travis himself had done; but all the actions of Dan Travis were odd. His greeting of Clancy had been strange. Put it down to the fact that a dead man was lying on the floor of his house at the moment. But the matter of the bandanna had been strange, too. It was so strange that Clancy Morgan wondered if Travis did not have a red bandanna, and if so, why it had not been given? The whole matter seemed to be focusing, suddenly, around the bandanna. A little wisp of silk—but a man might die because of it. He, Clancy Morgan, might die!

He rode on, dragging the horse of Orping behind him. On the veranda of the hotel stood old Culverson, with his shoulders stooped by weight and by years. He was talking in the midst of a group, but when he saw Clancy he paused and stared.

Then, like a flashing of metal toward the sun, all the other faces twisted around toward Morgan. There was a sudden loud talking of all the voices. It died out. In a silence in which he could hear the creaking of his stirrup straps, he approached the hotel, dismounted, and tethered Orping's horse to the rack. He tethered his own beside Orping's. The silence made him feel sick at his stomach. He walked around the watering troughs that bordered the veranda. Other men came in behind him. They followed him closely, and he dared not turn toward them, because he knew they were acting as part of a trap.

He knew every one of these people. He knew them intimately, and he had been away for a long time, but nobody spoke to him. He stood before old Culverson.

"Well," he said, "I've brought in the horse."

Culverson looked back at him and pursed his lips over his toothless mouth; then turned away. His old, bent back went slowly through the double doorway into the lobby of the hotel.

Clancy Morgan looked around him. Everybody met his eye coldly. Still nobody spoke.

"What's the matter?" asked Clancy Morgan. "What in the world is the matter?"

He wished Travis were at his side. He wished it very much. But Travis was somewhere in the background, making everything safe, preparing against every emergency. A sudden warmth of joy came upon the heart of Clancy, knowing he had such a friend as Travis in the background.

"Steve," said Clancy to Steve Pearson, "what's the matter?"

Steve Pearson was one of the best liked and respected men in town. He was only thirty, but he was gray from the scheming and work which had brought him up from utter poverty to the ownership of a very tidy herd. He was a little man—a big head and shoulders set on an almost dwarfish body. Now he looked into the face of Clancy Morgan with a steady disgust, a steady enmity.

"You must take us for a flock of fools, boy," said Pearson. "D'you think you can get away with this bluff?"

"What bluff?"

"You murdered Bill Orping," said Pearson.

"I—" gasped Clancy.

Pearson raised a hand slowly and leveled a forefinger that was like a gun. He came a step closer and said:

"You shot Bill Orping in the back!"

"I didn't! I—I—didn't!" exclaimed Clancy. "I just brought in his horse—I—"

"You brought in his horse. You thought doing that would prove you weren't afraid. You thought doing that would prove you were innocent, but we're not the sort of fools you take us for. We've lived a day or two."

"I know you have. I don't think you're fools," said Clancy Morgan. "Only, I tell you I didn't kill Bill Orping. I had nothing against him. We rode the same range together. We were on the same job. Everybody up there knows that Bill and I never had any trouble!"

Pearson sneered in his face. Those gray, relentless eyes kept boring into him.

"I have half a mind to go ahead," announced Pearson. "I think we *ought* to go ahead, boys. I don't see why we should wait for the sheriff to come two hundred miles. Tartartown has had clean hands for twenty years, and if her hands are dirty again, it's up to us to clean them!"

"It is," said another voice suddenly.

That was Jeff Rogers, with the face of a pig and the voice of a bear. Jeff was usually in the center of any crowd. He seemed to rise out of the ground and appeared as the nearest witness of any quarrel. Of course, he would be here!

Jeff flushed as the eye of Clancy found him.

"We oughta do the job ourselves," said Jeff loudly. "This here ladies' man and killer, we oughta handle him ourselves. He thinks we're a bunch of fools, but we'll show him another side of the face to laugh on!"

He shook his fat fist at Clancy.

Suddenly there was a stepping forward, as though a company of soldiers had heard a command, but all of those steps were toward Clancy. He was the magnet that drew the filings. He looked around him wildly, between heads and over heads, but Travis was not in sight.

Still, perhaps it didn't matter. Travis would appear at the right time. He could depend on Travis. Friendship was more than life to Travis. He was a man willing to stand up for his principles. He would fight for them, too! He would died for them! He would appear at the right time. That was what Clancy Morgan told himself.

"Pearson, you tell us what to do," said a man gravely.

"It's a dirty business," declared Pearson, "but I guess it's our duty. If we pass this up, we'll have a flock of thugs and yeggs and crooks coming down here and making themselves at home. For my part, if my own brother did a murder, I'd sit on the jury and vote for him to hang."

He snapped his teeth on the finish of this.

"Take him out under that tree!" commanded Pearson.

Hands fell on Clancy.

Then overmastering hysteria swept over him. He struggled to cast the hands off. They merely became ten times stronger, and the finger tips sank into his flesh.

''Wait a minute!'' screamed Clancy Morgan. ''I didn't kill him. Don't murder me, boys!''

''Take it like a man,'' said a voice at his ear. ''Take it like a man, if there's any man in you.''

And he was swept forward until he stood under the single tree that graced Tartartown and the plains around it, a single big cottonwood that rose like a green tower.

CHAPTER 5
Friendship

ALL AROUND HIM THE CROWD MOVED. IT WAS LIKE ONE huge, shapeless beast, moving on many pairs of feet, but with only a single heart, a single brain—and that heart and brain devising evil. Tentacles stronger than those of an octopus embraced Clancy Morgan. His life and soul were about to be devoured by this monster. He heard the voice of the crowd, too. It came from many throats, but it made a single deep, murmuring note. There was music in it— the sort of music that freezes the heart.

Something whispered in the air above the head of Clancy. He looked up and saw a lariat dangling close to him. Jeff Rogers had thrown it. Jeff was importantly hold-ing the end of the rope now, with a severe frown on his face, like one who is an executor of justice.

"Clear away a circle," said Pearson. "Stand back, boys. If this job has to be done, we'll try to do it decently. Stand away from him so we can ask him a few questions and see his face."

They stood back, and Clancy Morgan looked up and down the street. There was no sign of Dan Travis, but at the same time he felt certain Travis was somewhere near. Friendship was sacred to Travis. Friendship was more than life or death to him. Clancy knew that. The words became a chant audible to his mind's ear: "Friendship is sacred!"

He, Clancy Morgan, would prove it, even if the rope was fastened around his neck. Old Danny Travis would see there was one man in the world who agreed with him—friendship is sacred!

Might it not be, after all, that that man of cold nerve, Dan Travis, was somewhere nearby, waiting until the last moment, testing the courage of Clancy, ready to rescue him at the very last instant of danger?

As the thought occurred to Clancy, he was certain it was the correct solution. And he was steadied.

"We'll need Culverson here," said Pearson. "Get Culverson, will you?"

"Culverson won't come," said another. It was Tom Briggs. Tom had been in school with Clancy. They had punched each other in many a fight. They had raced together for the swimming pool after days of school in summer. But here was Tom Briggs, looking at him as though he never had seen him before, narrowing his eyes, curling his lip a little.

"Culverson won't come," repeated Tom Briggs. "He says the business makes him sick. And he looks as though he means it. He just tells how the dog found the body, and he went into the brush after it. There's one thing more. He says when he showed the bandanna he found there, he saw a very odd look on Clancy Morgan's face. That's all. He won't come here and talk."

"He's a decent old codger," declared Pearson. "But I hope the rest of us are decent men, too. If there's one of you all who has any malice against Clancy Morgan, I wish he'd step out of this. It's a dirty business, but we owe it to the honor and the safety of our town to put it through.

It's not so much what's happening now as what may happen in the future. Morgan!''

He snapped out the name. Clancy Morgan stiffened. He looked straight back into the stern face of Pearson. He stubbornly told himself that friendship was sacred. It was worth dying for. And a sort of glory came upon Clancy Morgan and cast the trembling out of his body, and enabled him to raise his head and look steadily back at Pearson.

On the edge of the crowd was the sober, middle-aged face of Olivia's father. Harry Gregor looked merely thoughtful—hardly concerned! Clancy's heart fell. But his mind was made up.

"Well, Morgan," said Pearson, "we want the straight of this. It seems you rode for the same outfit Bill Orping worked for. What bad blood came up between you? We'll start there!"

"No bad blood," said Clancy. He rejoiced in the wonderful steadiness of his voice.

"All right," said Pearson. "We can't make you talk. But we can hang you if you don't. We can hang you for a dirty murderer from a branch of this tree, and we've got the rope ready. Remember that!"

Clancy Morgan lifted his head and looked at the dangling rope.

"I understand," said he.

"Very well," said Pearson. "When did Orping leave your outfit? Will you tell us that?"

"He left just after sunset last night."

"When did you leave it?"

"Just at moonrise last night."

"And you rode straight down here—it's a long way!"

"I rode all night."

"Where did you go then?"

"I went to the house of Dan Travis."

"And what did you find there—or what did you do?"

"I won't tell you."

38

The shock went through every man in the crowd. Clancy could see them stir under the impact of it.

"You won't talk beyond that point?" asked Pearson.

"No," said Clancy.

"He won't talk," said Pearson. "So I'll have to present the case we have against him. These are the facts the way we know them, partly from what he says himself and partly from what other people have said. Orping left that ranch last night. He rode down to Tartartown. He was seen passing through the edge of town early this morning. And he was found dead in the mesquite outside of the house of Dan Travis. Dan Travis says he heard two shots fired this morning, and didn't leave his house to find out who fired them. Well, we'll let that go. We know Dan Travis, and we know he'd die for a friend. What Dan Travis says about this case isn't worth a tinker's damn, but as a matter of fact, even what Dan says is no good. Most of you heard him talk. He simply says he heard the shots. He thought nothing of them. After a while his friend Clancy Morgan arrived."

"That's right," said Jeff, nodding his head so that his pig jowls wabbled.

"Culverson testifies—and you know Culverson is not a man to lie—that he got to the house early, and that his dog found the body, and that when he went out to it, Culverson found a bandanna, a red silk bandanna, hanging on the edge of a mesquite thorn. He saw Clancy Morgan, and Clancy was wearing a blue-and-white bandanna. Mrs. Culverson remarked on it. And now comes the final thing. Half a dozen people saw Clancy Morgan ride through town this morning. He wasn't wearing a blue bandanna then. He was wearing a red one.

"Now, gentlemen, I'm going to put it up to you straight and fair. What happened? Did the murderer leave his bandanna at the place the body was found? Had it been stained, perhaps, so that he left it there? Or did he forget it, and afterward borrow one of Travis's blue-and-white affairs? I say, there's our argument, and here's a prisoner who won't talk past the time and the place where the murder was committed. Clancy, why don't you make a clean breast of it? If you'll do that, we'll promise to leave you to the law!''

''No!'' bawled Jeff. ''We've got him, and we're goin' to hang the dirty dog.''

''Shut up, Jeff,'' commanded Pearson. ''Clancy, will you talk?''

''No,'' said Clancy Morgan.

''Very well, then,'' said Pearson. ''You'll take the consequences. Gentlemen, if there's a single one of you who thinks Clancy is not guilty, I want him to speak up.'' A dead silence followed.

But it was not incomprehensible to Clancy.

Not one of them—not even his schoolmates raised a voice. He knew why. Even a killing can be forgiven in a country where weapons are commonly worn; but not a cowardly assassination. And Bill Orping had been shot through the back!

That was the crux of the thing.

''Very well,'' said Pearson. ''I say he's guilty. Nobody speaks to the contrary, but first I'll have a show of hands to—''

''You can't hang him,'' said the voice of Harry Gregor.

Everyone shifted. Gregor came through the crowd, and he looked to Clancy like a divine angel—a middle-aged angel, and therefore a wiser one.

''You can't hang him,'' he repeated.

''You can't stop us!'' replied Jeff loudly.

''I know every man jack of you,'' said Harry Gregor. ''You fellows can't do this, and I'm here to tell you. I know you, and unless you hang me with Clancy Morgan, I'll have *you* hanged afterward. Every man jack of you! You hear me?''

''It's a bluff!'' shouted Jeff. ''Throw him out, Pearson! Out with him, boys.''

"Throw me out, then," said Harry Gregor, "and hang your man. And the law will hang *you* for it later. You hear me, all of you? I'm not afraid of you, my lads. I'm not afraid of you, Pearson. You hear me? Take your hands from Clancy Morgan till the law wants him. And he'll be in Tartartown waiting for the law when it says the word."

"It's no will of mine to have a hand in this," said Pearson. "But a man was shot in the back, and that's dirty work."

"Look after your own life, young man," said Gregor. "Put an eye on your own affairs and you'll have enough to do. There's none of us so good he can afford to waste his time beating others. Not one of us! Take your hands from Clancy Morgan, the rest of you. Clancy, come along with me."

In all of this Gregor had not raised his voice. Had he ventured to do so, perhaps the charm would have been broken. For it was his calm and matter-of-fact way of speaking that held the rest of them in check and seemed to mock them with folly and rashness. All the life went out of the mob. Its voice died down to a muttering.

Pearson merely said: "The law will have its say."

"The law will have its say, young man," said Gregor. "And you'll be no part of the law, either. There may be a day when you'll groan for this, Pearson."

Pearson stood mute. Clancy and Gregor had passed from the limits of mob when Jeff began to bawl out something with his roaring voice. But the strength of the many-footed beast was gone. To Clancy it was like passing from death to life again. The very burn of the sun on his shoulders was a blessing. The hot, dusty wind was sweet in his nostrils.

"How did you know I didn't kill poor Orping?" asked Clancy.

"I didn't know it. I don't know it now," said Gregor gruffly. "But a friend's a friend!"

It was a strange thing to Clancy—almost a miracle. "Friendship is sacred" had been the chant in his ears. And a friend had saved him from so many hands.

CHAPTER 6
He'll Face It

"THEY MAY MISS YOU TODAY AND CATCH YOU TOMOR-row," said Gregor. "Get out of Tartartown and stay out."

"I'll see Olivia first," said Clancy.

"If she thinks you've shot a man in the back, she'd rather see the devil, horns and all, than you," said Gregor.

Clancy stopped short.

Looking behind him, he saw the dust rise over the still milling crowd of lynchers. It was true that there might be malice in them still. What they could not manage with naked faces today they might very well accomplish with masked faces tonight. And there was a deep anger in them or else they would have scattered, or begun to scatter, the instant they lost their victim.

Glancing about him, Clancy Morgan wondered where Travis had been all this while.

"I shot no man in the back," said Clancy Morgan.

"You say so," said Gregor, "but the evidence is all against you. If you're innocent, why didn't you speak out and tell them every move you'd made?"

"Because something kept me from it," said Clancy.

"Something more important than the safety of your neck?" snapped Gregor.

Clancy considered.

"Yes," he said at last. "Something more important than my neck."

"Well," answered Gregor, "go find Olivia if you want. But she may have her mind made up, and she's a stubborn girl, and her mother was a stubborn woman before her."

Clancy Morgan said: "I wish you'd tell me how you feel about this."

"I feel like the very devil about it," said the other, "if you really want to know."

"You really think I'm the guilty man?" asked Clancy bitterly.

There was infinite kindness in the face of Harry Gregor, but there was a stern manliness, also, and now he said: "Don't ask me again how I feel or what I think. The fact is, you're probably guilty, or all of those boys back there wouldn't be so keen to hang you. And mind you, Clancy, a thing they're afraid to do in the daytime they won't be afraid to do at night. That's all. I advise you to get out of this part of the country while the getting's good. But you're your own boss!"

Clancy Morgan went back to his tired horse. He did not climb into the saddle, but untied the horse and led it down the street and toward the eastern edge of the little town, where Gregor's house stood. Gregor himself went by him at a gallop, and did not speak as he flashed by. The dust clouds from the hoofs of that running horse laid a powdering of gray over Clancy.

He came up to the ranch house with its long-extending front, and went around it to the kitchen door.

"Hey, Nancy!" he called.

The Negress came to the door and poked out her head.

"Oh, Mr. Clancy, Mr. Clancy!" she cried, and wagged her head at him.

43

Nancy had heard everything, too, and even Nancy could not believe in him!

"Where's Olivia?" he asked.

"I wouldn't know," said Nancy solemnly. "I wouldn't know where she is."

"Is she in the house?"

"No, Mr. Clancy, she ain't in the house."

He turned impatiently and strode off toward the barn, pulling the mustang after him. She might be near the barn with one of her horses, or in the corrals behind it, for half her time seemed to be spent healing sick animals, or teaching clever ones new tricks.

As he rounded the corner of the barn, he saw Olivia riding off at a full gallop.

"Olivia!" he shouted.

He saw her head twitch part way around to look at him, but she rode on.

"Olivia!" he called out again, furiously, and sick with grief.

She checked the horse, seemed to hesitate, and then rode straight back to him.

She had an eye as direct as her father's and now he saw that it could also be as stern. She did not smile as she approached. She gave him the most matter-of-fact kind of greeting. Grief and shame and weakness mastered him. He could not say a word. The size of his own swelling heart choked him.

"Your father's talked to you and told you about things?" he asked her.

"Yes," said the girl.

"You were running away so you wouldn't have to see me?"

She hesitated, but answered honestly: "Yes."

"I wish you'd get down out of the saddle. I could talk to you better," said Clancy. "Or if you want, go on and ride away. Maybe it'll make you feel better."

"No, I'll stay. I shouldn't have tried to cut and run," she admitted.

She swung down out of the saddle and stood at the shoulder of her pony. She was making herself look him in the eye, but the effort told. She was prettier than he had thought—a great deal. Now that an invisible wall was raised between them, he could see more clearly how charming she was. She had also the simplicity and directness of a man about her. She was waiting for him to say something. It was hard to begin. Now that she was standing on the ground, he wished her back in the saddle.

"Why did you want to go?" he asked.

"I was afraid to see you," she answered. "I knew I'd be all cut up."

"Because you believe I'm a cowardly dog who would shoot a man in the back. That's it?"

She looked straight back at him and said nothing. He could feel the effort she was making.

"All right," said Clancy Morgan. "All I know is I won't try to argue you out of it. I came here—I came out here," he went on, fighting to keep his voice level, "because I wanted to say something to you, Olivia. You knew what I wanted to say, and you cut and run."

She still waited. He had to force her to talk by asking: "Didn't you guess what I would say?"

"You wanted to say that you're sort of fond of me," said the girl. She was rather pale around the mouth and dark about the eyes, he thought.

"That's what I wanted to say," answered Clancy Morgan. "I wanted to say that you've been in my head all the time I've been away from Tartartown. I wanted to say that I love you, Olivia. Does that make any difference to you?"

"I've been guessing at it," she answered. "But it makes a difference having you say it." She added honestly, with another effort: "A lot of difference!"

"Enough to make you care for me?" he asked her, beginning to come closer by inches.

"Everybody cares for you, Clancy," she said. "I suppose you know that. Everybody has been loving you. All the girls—everybody."

"I don't think so," said Clancy Morgan. "And I don't care about the others. I never cared about any one except you, Olivia."

"You knew the others liked you," said Olivia. "We've all been out of our heads about you. We've all talked together and said what we thought of you. We weren't ashamed. You were like a flag or a mountain, or something like that—fine and right all the way through. We've laughed at one another because we were all so fond of you."

He put aside all her words with his hand.

"And now you don't care any more, Olivia?"

"I didn't say that."

"You do care?"

"Yes," she said, and began to breathe hard and look frightened. He came right up to her with a long step.

"Olivia," he said, "you care a lot. Somehow I'm sure of it."

"Yes, I care a lot," she said.

He put his arms around her. She leaned her head back against his horse. Her eyes were closed.

"Don't kiss me, Clancy."

"You want me to," said he.

"Yes, but don't do it."

"I won't," said Clancy. "I'm sorry I touched you."

He stepped back from her. He had loved her more than anything in the world before this, and now he respected her more than anything else.

She opened her eyes again and began to cry. There was no sobbing or trembling of the lips, but her eyes altered, and the tears went rapidly down her face.

"That's because of me," said Clancy. "That's because you think I'm a hound."

She said nothing. He took out a handkerchief and tried to dry her face, but the tears kept on coming.

"I'll tell you something," said Clancy Morgan, "I'll swear—"

"Don't!" she begged him. "Do anything else, but don't do that!"

"I was going to swear to you that I didn't—"

"Don't swear. That's what I couldn't stand."

"Olivia, you think I did it!"

"I don't know. I'm praying you didn't. I'm praying and hoping. Some day—I don't know—I might be able to feel that you were just young, that he frightened you out of yourself, maybe; that such a thing wasn't really in your heart, that it just sort of happened. Maybe I can feel that way about it sometime, but if you lie on top of everything else, I'll feel as though I've been loving a bad dog and not a man at all!"

He stood up to those last words with speech working and shuddering in his throat—the whole, true story of exactly what had happened. But she stirred him so with pity and with love, she seemed to him so noble, so gentle, and so true, that Clancy Morgan was forced into remembering another thing that was just as great and glorious—Dan Travis's conception of friendship.

Suddenly it seemed to Clancy that the future opened to him and showed him a golden time in which he would secure, in spite of all present dangers and darkness, the two priceless possessions of the world, a friend as tried and proved as steel, and the woman he loved.

An infinite quiet came over the mind of Clancy Morgan, a sad surety.

The girl said: "Father wanted me to say one thing to you. He wanted me to beg you to get out of Tartartown. He said the crowd didn't dare to go ahead after he'd challenged them because the daylight showed him all their faces. But he says that when night comes, with masks—''

"I'm not going away," said Clancy Morgan. "If I run away, I'd be a disgrace to everybody who ever cared a rap about me. I'm going back to see this thing through. For my own sake, and for your sake, too. Good-by, Olivia.''

Her lips stirred; she nodded; but no speech came.

Clancy left and went back, still leading the tired mustang, into Tartartown.

It was all changed, now. It looked to him as a battlefield looks to a soldier when the fight has commenced, but has not ended. The more familiar it was, the more grim.

The doctor came up the street, driving his light buggy, and nodded curtly at Clancy, without giving him a full glance. Jay Williams's two boys dashed, whooping, around a corner and stood transfixed when they saw him, as though they'd come upon a ghost.

In fact, he knew that he *was* a ghost to them, a man whose honor was gone, and therefore who was worse than dead, although he still was alive, to walk and talk and breathe the air with other men.

He came to the hotel and passed into it. There was still a dozen people about the lobby, and all of them stood up with a savage murmur when they saw him. He went to the desk. As he turned from the others, cold worms of fear crawled up and down his spine. The clerk looked at him for a long, deadly moment.

"Well," he said, "I suppose we've got to give you a room!''

He got up, snatched a key from a hook, and contemptuously led the way up the stairs.

And Clancy Morgan followed with his head high. This insult was nothing. It could be endured, and more insults, far worse, because every sacrifice he made was laid on the high altar of friendship. But it was strange, he felt, it was very, very strange that Danny Travis did not appear.

CHAPTER 7
True To Travis

CLANCY LOCKED THE DOOR WHEN THE CLERK HAD GONE out of the bedroom. It was a flimsy affair, that door. It looked as though even a boy could give it the weight of a lunging shoulder and knock it flat.

That made him get out his revolver. It was obviously dirty. It needed cleaning and oiling. So he rubbed off the dust and spun the cylinder to free it. Then he put the Colt back in its holster, looking at the door. Perhaps its six bullets would have to serve in lieu of stronger locks and bolts to shield him from his enemies.

He went to the window. There was a one-story drop to the ground. The eaves of another window projected just below him. A cat or a man like Travis might be able to climb up to his room by this route. Clancy was tired, and he felt he should be more rested when the crisis came. It would come that night, of course.

He pulled off his boots, stretched himself on the bed, and folded his hands under his head. In all the world there was no one like Olivia. She grew in his mind as the sun grows in a winter sky. She doubted and half despised him, she was tortured with pain on account of him, but she loved him. He considered the ache in his own heart impersonally. It was as though bullets had torn through him there; but still he lived on.

In another moment he closed his eyes and was asleep.

He wakened to hear a heavy thumping on the door. It seemed to have been going on for a long time.

"They've come to get me!" breathed Clancy Morgan, and jumped to his feet.

Then he saw that the afternoon sun was still slanting past the window, filling the air with an unusually bright haze.

"Who's there?" he called.

"Dan. Open up, boy!" said the voice of Travis.

Clancy Morgan inhaled a breath of life and opened the door. There was no one with Travis. He came into the room alone and closed and locked the door behind him.

Then he took Clancy by the arm, led him to the window light, and examined him. You would have said that he was a doctor looking over a convalescent patient.

He nodded.

"You're standing it," he said.

"Sure, I'm standing it," said Clancy Morgan. "Sit down. Want the makings?"

"Thanks," said Travis.

He sat in the rocking-chair, keeping it motionless, with his long, powerful legs stretched out before him. With a wheat-straw paper and tobacco, he made his cigarette, seeming to spill not a grain of the tobacco.

That was like Travis, thought Clancy, as he also rolled a cigarette. Everything Travis did he did perfectly. Think how he'd carved the under faces of the beams in his house! He could do anything, and do it perfectly. He was that sort of man. His face was both stern and serene. One might have called it savage, and there was indeed savagery in him. But not for Clancy.

The cigarettes were made. Clancy scratched a match and held it. They smoked in silence.

"What did you feel like in the crowd?" asked Travis, more like a doctor than ever.

It was a temptation to boast, but Travis was a man who could see through pretense as though it were of sheerest gossamer.

"I was scared," confessed Clancy. "I was scared to death. I think I yelled out, at first, a couple of times. I begged them not to kill me, I suppose." He flushed.

"And then toward the end, before Gregor stepped in?" asked Travis.

"Well, I thought about something that made me feel a lot better. It gave me surety and steadied my nerves. I wouldn't have stopped hoping even after they fitted the rope around my neck."

"What did you think of?" asked Travis gently.

"Of you, Danny," said Clancy, and flushed in another way.

Travis looked suddenly down at his cigarette and knocked off the ash.

"That fellow Gregor," said Travis, "is a man."

"He saved my life," said Clancy, self-pity and gratitude making his voice tremble.

"There aren't many people in the world I want to remember," said Travis slowly, softly. "Most of 'em I want to forget, and I *do* forget. But I want to remember Gregor. And I *shall* always remember him!"

There flashed before the mind of Clancy a picture of Gregor in frightful dangers, crowds of enemies rushing upon him in a stormy night, and then the terrible form of Travis riding to the rescue, sweeping Gregor off to warm life and safety. That was what Travis was, a true friend.

It was strange that when Travis said things like this, his face grew sterner than ever. He seemed to be speaking to himself rather than to another man.

"Now, about all the rest of it," said Travis. "Looks as though you're going to stay on in town?"

"Yes," said Clancy Morgan. "I've got to."

"Why do you have to? That's what I can't see."

"Because—well, because there's a girl around here who thinks I really shot poor Orping."

"Orping was a thug and yegg, as bad as his brother Jasper, but not so famous," corrected Travis without emotion.

"She thinks I shot him—through the back. I have to stay," said Clancy Morgan.

"Who's the girl?" asked Travis, his voice gentler than ever.

"You know the people of Tartartown pretty well by this time," said Clancy. "Who's the finest girl in town, bar none?"

"The prettiest?" asked Travis dreamily.

"Well, maybe not. I don't know. I mean the finest girl, the one with the best of the right stuff in her, that would see you through thick and thin. The sort of a girl that's easiest to imagine being a mother to your children, and a wife to you, and a friend to *your* friends."

"You'll never find a wife who'll like your friends," said Travis dryly.

"Well, maybe not. But you know what I mean. The best sort of a girl to make a woman—the very best in this place. Who would she be?"

"The Gregor girl," said Travis instantly.

"By Jove," said Clancy, "You hit it right the first guess. You *would* hit it right."

Travis leaned forward so far that his face was hidden, and knocked the ash from his cigarette outside the window sill. His head was still lowered while he asked in almost a yawning voice: "And what about her, Clan? How does she feel about it?"

"She thinks that I'm the sort of a rotten coward that will shoot a man in the back."

Travis straightened and puffed at his cigarette.

"Does she?" said he. Then he added: "Did I break up romance for you, Clan?"

"No," said Clancy Morgan. "She thinks I'm a rotten coward, but she loves me, anyway."

"Ah?" said Travis, and looked suddenly down at his cigarette again.

Joy suddenly sprang up out of the heart of Clancy Morgan.

"She told me so! It would have twisted your heart to see her and hear her, Danny. Ah, she stood there and cried, and said she loved me. I put my arms around her. She told me not to touch her. She said she loved me, and told me not to touch her. She cried, Dan!"

Clancy Morgan walked the floor. Travis looked down at his cigarette for a long time silently.

"She didn't sob," said Clancy, his voice shaking, lowered so that the tremor of it would be less perceptible. "Her lips didn't quiver, either. She just cried. The tears just rolled down her face."

"And then you told her?" said Travis.

"Told her what, Dan?"

"Told her the truth about everything?"

"What sort of a cur do you think I am, Dan? No, I didn't tell her. I love her, and I was tempted to tell her, I'll admit, but all at once I saw that unless I were man enough to be true to you, I was not man enough to be true to her. That was all. I didn't tell her anything. I just said I was coming back to Tartartown to face the music. It will keep her *hoping* I'm the right sort, no matter what she really thinks. She's the reason why I can't leave Tartartown."

He added: "And then, the whole thing will be cleared up, of course. It's worth going through, Dan. Just for the

53

sake of being able to go to her when all the clouds have blown away, and to see her face. I keep wondering. She'll nearly cry again. Lord, Dan, what a happy day that will be!"

"Yes," said Travis slowly. "What a happy day. But I wonder how it will be cleared up?"

"I don't know. Your brains are ten times better than mine. I know you're doing all a man can do to straighten it out."

"Now tell me just one thing, Clan."

"Fire away."

"Do you never doubt me?"

"Doubt you?" said Morgan.

"I mean, do you never suspect that I'm trying to get out from under and leave the whole weight of this on your shoulders? Things are fixed now so that I could, you know."

"Doubt you?" said Clancy Morgan. He tried to laugh, and almost managed to. "Why, Danny, what sort of a rat do you think I am? I know what you think of your friends, old fellow. I tell you what, Dan, next to Olivia, you're the top of the world for me. No, hardly next to her. Right up there beside her. I'd rather doubt myself than doubt you."

Travis stood up.

"You haven't even asked me what I'm doing, or planning to do," said he.

"Good old Dan," said Clancy Morgan. "What good would the asking do? I know that the old brain is working day and night. I know that your hand is on my shoulder all the time. You're right beside me."

Travis went up behind him as Clancy stood staring out the window at the brightness of the sun and the glory of his thoughts. He put both hands on the shoulders of Morgan and let them rest there for a moment. Then he went out of the room without saying a word.

CHAPTER 8
Attacked!

When Clancy had locked the door, he lay down again, but he could not sleep. He hardly needed sleep. There was such a tumult of happiness and resolution in his mind that he forgot his weariness.

Then he stood up as the chill in the air told him of sundown. He went to the dining room of the hotel and sat at a corner of the table. The whole length of the table was full. Most of the men there came from out of town. They had the dark red-brown of the open range, and Clancy knew why they had ridden in on this day.

A good many of them he knew and nodded to, but he was not surprised when they looked back at him without a sign of recognition. Their eyes simply ate him up angrily. The wind, or something else, seemed to have stained all of those eyes a dull yellow-red in the whites.

The sweet, sharp breath of whisky was in the air. They had all been drinking. But they had not been drinking enough to make their voices loud. Even when they asked that a platter be passed, they spoke softly. A funereal atmosphere was in the air. And it was not because the body of Bill Orping was stretched out in a room of the hotel. It was because they had come for the hanging of Clancy Morgan. He knew it as he sat there.

Yet it was clear they would not attempt anything for the moment. No, they had learned a lesson from Gregor—heard of what he'd done—on this day, and the next time they moved, their faces would be masked, and the murk of the night would help to cover them.

Where was the sheriff in the meantime? No doubt the telephone had carried a message far away, and the sheriff, by now, had turned the head of his horse toward Tartartown. But the county was as big as a kingdom, and he might be days in coming. The thing would be tragedy or comedy before that moment arrived.

Clancy Morgan finished his supper, pushed back his chair, and went out of the room. He knew all eyes were watching him, and as he passed into the outer hall he could hear a sudden clamorous outbreak as many voices were lifted behind him. Men cannot very well talk loudly and cheerfully in front of their chosen victim.

That instant he swore that so long as he lived, he would never judge other men harshly and suddenly. He went up to his room, locked the door once more, and got ready for bed. Probably they would try to break into his room that night, but it was hardly likely they would do so until they had gathered in greater force and had taken a little more whisky on board. For whisky sharpens the teeth of men and dulls their brains until they are like beasts. He could understand that now. There were a great many things he could understand now that had once been obscure to him.

He undressed, some cold water in the washbasin, and scrubbed his body clean. Then he shaved. The lean, brown face that looked back at him seemed, to the eyes of Clancy

Morgan, to show resolution and much determination. Well, he would need it all tonight.

Fear was not mastering him—either his body or his brain. To be sure, if he had to depend upon himself, he would have gone mad with terror. But in the background, supporting him, more formidable than an army, was the hand and brain of Dan Travis. When the pinch came, Travis would be there.

He was so certain of this that nine-tenths of the burden was taken from his shoulders. All he had to do was to hold up his end of the thing, as a true partner would be expected to do.

While he was dressing again, he heard the horses come down the street to the hotel and halt. One after one, and then in little groups, they were coming to the hanging of Clancy Morgan. And Clancy Morgan, having dressed, all except his boots, having shaken his door to prove that it was locked, pulled down the shade of his window.

Then he changed his mind and opened it again. They might be tempted to put a ladder up against a blinded window. They would not be apt to attempt an attack so long as it was open and a man with a gun somewhere inside.

Now he went to the lamp, took it off the table, and examined the height of the oil. It was nearly full, and should be able to burn all through the night. He turned down the wick a little and placed the lamp at one side of the door, near the wall. Around it he arranged two newspapers, folded so they stood up securely on edge.

When he had done this, he lay down on the bed again and looked about him.

The room was thick with darkness, except for one irregular spot of white on the ceiling, just above the lamp. When he was sure everything was arranged, he put the revolver beside him and fell asleep.

He was amazed when he wakened, to discover that he

had actually slept. But now he heard a steady, strong trampling of feet that came up the stairs and poured down the
hallway. It was not a rapid flood, but it was strong enough
to sweep away his life, perhaps.

Where was Dan Travis now?

He looked toward the window half expecting to see the
head and strong shoulders of his friend appear, but there
was a jet-black square of night and nothing more.

He strode to the window.

Outside, in the street, he could make out three dim sil-
houettes. No, they were taking no chances. They had
blocked him in on every side. If he strove to climb down
from the window, he would be shot to pieces on the way.
Or perhaps those fellows down there would prefer to catch
him alive, for the lynching was what they wanted, to see
the death and the fear in his face as the rope settled around
his neck.

How could they know, poor fools, that Dan Travis understood all about this, and in the wisdom of his mind was
preparing some perfect counterstroke?

Clancy Morgan actually smiled.

Perhaps Travis himself would appear in the hallway
when the crowd drew near the door. Yes, as the trampling
footfalls approached the door, Clancy more than half expected to hear the stern voice of Danny Travis ring out
with a challenge, threatening them, perhaps, with a riot
gun.

But no voice rang out. There was only a sudden and
terrible beating of many hands against his door.

He stepped to the lamp and drew away that newspaper
which kept the light from shining on the door. Now it
threw a big, strong wedge of illumination across that side
of the room.

"Who's there?" called Clancy Morgan.

"A reception committee!" bawled out a voice.

Laughter followed.

"Stop that laughing," said the voice of Pearson. "Any man who takes this for a joke is a fool. This is justice, not a game!"

Clancy lay down in the darkest corner of the room, stretched out on his stomach, and steadying his revolver with both hands, he drew a careful bead on the door, breast-high.

"Open this door, Morgan," said Pearson. "We've come for you, and we're going to get you!"

A sudden frenzy rushed up into the brain of Clancy Morgan. He did not recognize the shrill voice that came tearing against his ears, but it was his own.

"You dirty, murdering cowards! Get back from that door or I'll pile you up dead on the sill!"

"Break it down, boys," said the calm voice of Pearson.

Instantly there was a heavy crash. The door flew wide and slammed against the wall. The whole room trembled, but not the hands of Clancy Morgan.

Perhaps Dan Travis was at this moment looking in at the window, ready to mow some of that crowd down. In the meantime, he, Clancy Morgan, would do his honest share! He fired straight into the dimly entangled forms which his eyes discovered.

He won a yelping of pain from two distinct voices. The three men who had started to rush through the open door recoiled in haste, flinging themselves back, having to fight to get away because of the pressure behind them.

Now, it would be a poorly aimed bullet that did not take at least one life out of that heap of humanity.

"Get back! Let me get out! He's shooting us! Kill him!"

They put up a roar of shouts but fell back from before the doorway.

Clancy Morgan, filled with a wild, dizzying exultation, shouted to them: "Come on! There's a crowd of you! there's a whole crowd! I'm only one man. I'm the coward, you say, who shot a fellow through the back. Now let me see how brave you are. You, Pearson, who loves the law so much, let me see you do something about it, you rotten coward!''

A man was groaning in the hallway: ''My leg's broken. I'm ruined for life. My leg's smashed all to the devil!''

Another was cursing wildly. A whole volley tore into the room, but not a bullet came within yards of Morgan. They could not spot him. They had a flood of light turned into their faces, and the newspaper behind the lamp placed the other half of the room in utter blackness. They could not even shoot out the lamp without exposing themselves.

''Try again, boys,'' said Clancy Morgan, ''and take this for good measure!''

He fired, not through the doorway, which he knew wasn't filled, but at the flimsy wooden wall to one side of the door. It would hamper the crowd in the hall, but it would not hamper a Colt's .45-caliber bullet.

The slug snicked through the wall as though it were paper. He had purposely aimed only hip high. A wild yelling greeted the shot, and he knew it had clipped the flesh of more than one man.

A savage joy swept over Clancy and made him hot from head to foot.

''Scatter, scatter; don't stand so close together!'' commanded Pearson in the hall.

''It's a hell hole! It's a death trap!'' roared another voice, which sounded very like that of Jeff Rogers. ''Get out of here and save yourselves, boys!''

''Stand tight!'' yelled Pearson. ''Don't run, you fools, you cowards! Stand fast and be men!''

''Be men and be dead!'' cried Clancy Morgan. ''Let's see the quality of you heroes who love the law so much! Let's see the sort of men who do the lynching in the name of the law in this town! You rats, why don't you fight?''

But there was only a long, receding roar of voices and footfalls as the herd swept down the hallway.

The passion in young Clancy Morgan, and the incredulous joy of his sudden delivery, made him leap into the doorway. He saw the crowd huddling together as it stampeded, one man crying out that his leg was being twisted off his body, and another that he was being crushed to death, and another asking help to carry one of the wounded. But not a soul turned to fight the battle out, not even Pearson, who retreated at the heels of the others, cursing them, reviling them.

Clancy Morgan let out a wordless roar like that of a beast of prey. He put two bullets over the heads of the crowd and two bullets under their feet, and they pitched headlong down the stairs with such a thundering that the very vibration of the sound seemed sufficient to burst the hotel apart.

There was not another bullet in his gun, but he had a distinct feeling he would not need another.

He let the door stand open with its broken lock, blew out the lamp, and stretched himself once more on his bed. Outside he could hear voices raging up and down the scale, but he felt certain he had nothing more to fear that night. He went to sleep with only one wonder in his mind.

Where had Travis been?

CHAPTER 9
A Girl's Warning

WHEN HE WOKE THE SUN WAS SHINING. HE WASHED and stood a moment at the window, looking out. The sun seemed to make the whole world anew, and his life with it.

Last night had been a dream, this morning was reality. They could not hold malice against him because he had fought for his life. On the contrary, they might put two and two together, perhaps, and come to the conclusion he was not exactly the type of fellow to shoot another through the back.

But what should he do now?

Well, he was hungry, and the smell of cookery was in the air. Without further thought, he broke open his empty gun, grinned at its emptiness, and then went straight down to the dining room, with the empty Colt moving in its holster against his hip.

In the dining room he found a dozen others. They looked as though they had not slept. The whisky flush or the whisky pallor was in their faces. When they saw him, they simply looked down at their plates or into their cups of coffee.

Clancy Morgan sat at the end of the table, with his back to the wall, and ate with the others. Not a one of them, he could be sure, had been absent from the crowd of the night before. And not a one of them dared look him in the face!

After breakfast he went into the lobby.

Other men were there. Studiously they avoided him.

"Anyone seen my friend Pearson?" asked Clancy Morgan.

The answer was silence and gloomy staring at the floor.

He stepped to the desk, where the clerk was immensely busy with a pile of papers, shuffling them, arranging them, and then rearranging them.

"Give me a room with a lock on the door that isn't broken," said Clancy, "and have my stuff moved into it—my blanket roll."

"Yes. Certainly," said the clerk, and did not look up from his papers.

Clancy Morgan stepped out into the sunshine of the street. It felt quite different from any sunshine he ever had known before. He could almost taste it. And the air was of an incredible sweetness.

He went to the general store. Old Sam Hilton was behind the counter, he looked startled, half frightened, when he saw Morgan.

"I want a box of .45s and some oil," said Clancy.

Hilton turned to the shelf holding ammunition. His withered hands hesitated for a long time. Then he took down a small cardboard box and pushed it across the counter.

"How are things, Mr. Hilton?" asked Clancy Morgan.

The old man shook his head slowly.

"Things are mighty bad for some people in this town," said he. "Mighty bad, mighty bad!"

Clancy went into the street, walked to the end of it, and slowly returned.

What should he do? Where was Travis?

Back at the hotel, waiting for him, perhaps.

He hurried a little and turning the corner toward the hotel, he saw a cortege of hatless men stepping slowly along, followed by a silent crowd. Eight were carrying a coffin draped in black with a few flowers thrown upon it. Bill Orping's body was going to its grave.

Clancy Morgan stood back and took off his hat.

No one looked at Clancy. Their eyes seemed riveted straight before them, upon the unhappy mysteries of this life. They stepped carefully. Their feet did not seem to raise the dust. There was not a woman among them.

No, the women were standing on their porches, or they were at their windows, watching.

So Clancy, with bared head, watched the procession move gradually past him. Then he walked on toward the hotel.

He was in No. 17 now, the clerk told him. No. 17 was the best room in the house, on the corner overlooking two streets. Two windows, thought Clancy, through which bullets could be fired.

But perhaps the brave men of Tartartown would not be firing bullets for a while. Perhaps they had enough of shooting to last them for a time.

He sat down before the window. The day was growing hot. Noises came to him of labor, the clanking hammers in the blacksmith shop, the squeaking of a saw from the direction of the repair job on the old Quincy house, and some woman with a high voice bargaining or scolding at Sid Wilson, the grocer, just across the street.

Everybody else in this world was busy, but for his own part, he sat still and waited for the current to bear him along.

A footfall hurried to his door. There was someone downstairs to see him.

He looked to his freshly loaded gun, pulled his sombrero firmly down over his eyes, and walked downstairs. In the lobby, Olivia Gregor stood up to meet him. They were virtually alone. Only the clerk was seemingly quite busy with odds and ends.

"Are you going to stay, Clancy?" she asked him, her face non-commital, her voice almost expressionless. "I heard that you hadn't left. Are you really going to stay?"

"I'm going to stay," said Clancy Morgan a little proudly. "Why not? I don't think they'll try to mob me again."

She shook her head. "I've heard all about that."

She watched him.

"Clan," she said, "if you could do a thing like that—"

She stopped, and he narrowed his eyes to watch her. She must have driven in, because she was wearing a dress of a rough blue silk. He knew it was the most beautiful dress in the world. She had on a blue hat, with a tuft of yellow flowers against the crown.

"Well," she went on, "I won't talk about it."

"Have you given up hoping that maybe I didn't shoot Orping in the back?" asked Clancy Morgan bluntly.

"If I stopped hoping, I think I'd die. No, I'm still hoping. They tell me you're looking for Pearson?"

"Pearson was the ringleader twice," said Clancy Morgan.

"Will you promise me something?" she asked.

"Yes, anything except that I run out of town."

"It's only this: stop looking for Pearson."

"All right, I'll stop, if it makes you happier. Why should it, though?"

"He was jealous, Clancy. That's all I can tell you."

"He wanted you? That's what was behind all this talk about the law?"

"He was jealous, I'm afraid. But don't look for him. You've promised me that you won't."

"Pearson, too!" said Clancy Morgan. "Aren't there any more honest men in the world? Olivia, there's nobody under the sun I can bank on except Dan Travis. And the next thing I know *he'll* be falling in love with you. That's what he'll be doing."

She started. "Does Dan Travis mean more to you than any other friend, Clan?"

"Dan? Of course he does! A great deal more."

"Well—" she said, and then paused, looking rather miserably up at him.

"Go on," said he, frowning. "Only don't go far enough to say anything against Dan. I know he's been a rough fellow and done some rough things, and perhaps there was a time in his life when he shot a little too straight and a little too often. But he's a man, Olivia—and he's my friend."

"Well," she said slowly, studying him all the time, "isn't it a little strange he wasn't on hand last night? Poor Dad heard the racket, and came rushing to the hotel. But everything was over then. He just saw—the wounded! Joe Breck has a broken leg, and Will Porter—Well, dad was surprised to find that Dan Travis hadn't been there to help you. Were *you* surprised?"

He flushed very hot.

"There'll be plenty of explanation," said Clancy Morgan. "You'll see. There'll be plenty of explanation. Why, Dan is the Rock of Gibraltar. I love him, Olivia. So would you if you knew him."

"I know him pretty well," she said with the same cautious slowness of speech, as though she were afraid her words would give away too much of her thought. "I know him pretty well. And I could never love him, Clancy."

"That's the woman of it!" exclaimed Clancy Morgan bitterly. "Because he looks hard, because he *is* hard, in a way, you won't see he's the finest fellow in the world. I'll tell you what, even if I were better than anything you ever thought about me, or wished about me, I wouldn't be much compared to a man like Dan Travis!"

She looked long and earnestly at him. "I love you," she said suddenly, "and, somehow, I feel that I may lose you."

"You won't," he told her. "Will you come outside with me?"

"No, I'm going to say good-by. You've made up your mind you'll wait here? You won't go away, Clan?"

"No. I'm staying till my name is cleared as bright as a mirror. And it will help me clear it."

"Do you want to know something?" she asked him gravely.

"Go on."

"Dan Travis would like to see you dead at his feet!"

The shock of it staggered him. Then he drew himself up.

"I'll tell you what, Olivia, I'm sorry you said that. I want you to know friendship is a sacred thing to me. And Dan—he's away up with me. He's next to you! After you've said that, he's *above* you! He—he'd rather die than slander a friend! I'll tell you one thing that'll burn you up with shame—he thinks you're the finest woman he knows. He said it. He said it in my own room yesterday. Olivia, he—"

Clancy stopped.

"And he *will* see you dead at his feet when Jasper Orping gets here today! Don't you understand? Oh, Clancy, my heart's breaking!"

When his eyes cleared, when he was able to look up, he saw that she had left him.

Chapter 10
Travis's Play

Clancy went into the barroom. No one was there but the bartender, who was washing glasses, drying them on a soiled cloth. He put his wet hands on top of the bar and waited for the order.

"Whisky, Pete," said Clancy Morgan.

"Yeah. That's what I thought," said Pete.

He was a sawed-off little man, famous for his savagery in a fight. He rolled out a bottle and a glass and stood with his head bent down, looking up from under his fleshy brow at Clancy Morgan, who was filling the glass.

"Whisky would have been pretty good last night, too, eh?" said Pete.

Morgan threw the liquor down his throat. The sour, sick taste of it rose again. Then the smoke and the fire went up into his nostrils. He felt all his frozen blood start with a leap.

"Some of them dumbbells, they got some new thinks in the think-tank today," said Pete. "Some of 'em is goin' to lie in bed, and think for quite a spell. Four of 'em is goin' to do that."

He added savagely: "I wouldn't join a mob. A mob is a lot of howlin' dogs. If I got a grudge, I take it out with my own hands. I don't want no help. They don't come too big for me. Even *you* ain't too big for me!"

Clancy Morgan gripped the edge of the bar, thinking of Jasper Orping, with all the ghosts of his dead men riding behind him, bound for Tartartown, reaching it on this day!

There was Dan Travis, of course, but even Dan, with his lightning hand and sure aim, what was Dan Travis compared with that conjuring devil of a Jasper Orping?

"You hear me, kid?" repeated Pete, as if trying to tell him something important. "*You* ain't too big for me, if *I* had a grudge. I cut 'em down to my own size. I whittle 'em down."

"I know," said Clancy Morgan vaguely.

He looked around the barroom, stifling in it as in a closet, threw down his money and went back into the lobby. There he got pen and paper and wrote:

> *Dear Dan*
> *Have you heard? Hell is loose! Jasper Orping is expected back this very day. Come and tell me what we're to do. I'm worried.*
>
> > *Clancy.*

He sealed it and went to the clerk.

"Give some kid a quarter," he said, sliding over the money, "and let him take this out to Dan Travis, will you?"

"Certainly, Mr. Morgan," said the clerk, looking down.

Of course, they looked down, for they knew what the girl knew; that Jasper Orping was coming to town. And he, Clancy Morgan, was to stay and face him!

He was choking. He touched his throat and felt the silk of the bandanna. He would have to die, along with Travis, because he was wearing a blue-and-white bandanna!

And then he grew whiter. Olivia, to be sure, had said good-by to him as though already he were a dead man, but that was because she placed no faith in Dan Travis. She actually did not like him! He considered this fact grimly. It meant that she was not really a thoroughbred or she would have seen the greatness of Travis.

Well, Travis had said that no woman could like a man's friends. He was right. He was always right. He was truly and surely right when he swore that friendship is sacred.

Clancy Morgan went up to his room and waited. His whole body was trembling. Then he heard footfalls and the voice of Travis in the hall.

He snatched the door open and caught at Travis with both hands. Travis halted and looked down at the hands that held him. Clancy released him. He must never forget the grim reserve that hedged Dan Travis. He was ashamed of the excitement that had overmastered him.

As they stood in the room, he said: "You got my note, Dan?"

"Well, I'm here."

"Good old Dan!" said Clancy Morgan. "And you know what I've heard?"

"What?"

"Nothing," said Morgan, thinking of the girl's words. If she could see them now together, perhaps even she would understand what man can be to man.

"Jasper Orping is coming," said Travis, sitting down, "and he'll be looking for you because you have on one of my bandannas. How do you feel, Clan?"

"Rotten. Ready to break all up—to go to pieces."

"I'll bet you do," said Travis, eyeing him curiously. He put out his long, narrow jaw a little. It was like the jaw of a bull terrier, and like the lips of a bull terrier were the thin, sardonic lips of Travis. He was not a pretty man.

"I'll bet you feel rotten, boy. And no wonder. Jas has a pretty big reputation in this old world, eh?"

"He's a dead shot," said Clancy Morgan.

"Rot!" said Travis, and snapped his fingers. "Dead shot? There's no man in the world that's a dead shot."

He considered, and snapped his fingers again without speaking.

"All I want is the plan," said Clancy Morgan. "I'll try to do my part."

"A big reputation is what he has," said Travis. "But I'll tell you what, Clan, the best of us lose our reputations sometimes. One dead Jasper Orping will be enough to wipe out his fine record."

Morgan nodded.

"I'll do whatever you tell me to do, Dan," said he. "But I guess it wouldn't be right and fair for both of us to stand up to him?"

"Hold on," said Travis. "Two against one? Is that what you mean?"

"Well," said Clancy Morgan, "I was just saying it wouldn't be fair."

"Fair?" said Travis. "It would be murder! I've killed men in my time, but murder, that's a different thing."

"I know, Dan," agreed Morgan. "I know you're as straight as a ruled line."

"I'm not as straight as a ruled line. Only—murder—it's different!"

He contemplated the idea of it, and his upper lip curled a little, as though in disgust.

"I'm not for crooked work, either," said Clancy Morgan. "I'm for anything you say is the right way. That's all."

"You're not for crooked work, but you're only a kid," said Travis.

"I know," said Clancy.

"They pulled one almost over on me last night," said

71

Travis thoughtfully. "I hadn't figured it for such an early break. More about midnight, was what I was sure of. But they didn't get you. The point was, however, I should have been there."

"I knew that would worry you. Forget it," said Clancy. "I worked a dodge on them, and they ran."

He laughed a little.

"I know. You beat 'em out. You have nerve, Clan. You have cold nerve. You're only a kid, but you have cold nerve. You ran the devil right out of them."

He said this soberly, as one who speaks only after mature judgment.

"I had luck," said Clancy Morgan, growing bright red with pleasure.

"There's no luck but bad luck when it comes to one man against a crowd," said Travis. "A couple of years on you, Clancy, and you'll be able to look any man in the eye. Don't answer me. I'm just telling you. You'll be able to stand up to anyone. But that's not what I want for you. I want a quiet life for you. A married life and children. I don't want you to step out into the hell fire. I've been there. I know what it's like."

Clancy Morgan sat like a stone. He never before had heard his friend talk like this, talk as to an equal.

"I should have been here last night!" muttered Travis.

"Don't think about it, Dan."

"Don't tell me not to think of it. I'll think of it the rest of my life. It was a mistake. I played the fool. I should have been here. Lord, Clan, they might have killed you!"

He reached out suddenly and put his hand over the hand of Morgan, and looked painfully, deeply, into his eyes.

"They didn't kill me. I'm all right," said Clancy, flushing again. For he saw that Travis seemed deeply moved. He felt unworthy of this demonstration. It frightened him a little.

Travis said: "Go down and get your horse and ride out to my shack."

"You mean you're going to stay in town and face him all by yourself when he comes through, Danny?"

"Don't ask me what I mean to do. Just do as I say."

Clancy Morgan rose slowly to his feet.

"I ought not to," he said. "I'll feel like a coward the rest of my life."

"Why? You're not hiding. If anybody asks where you're going, you tell 'em. There's nothing hidden about this. You're not sneaking away. If anybody asks you, just tell 'em you're going out to my cabin."

"You really want me to go?"

"Clan, don't stay and argue with me. Let me use the little brain that the Almighty gave me without making an argument all the time."

Clancy Morgan went to the door.

"I'll tell you what you are, Danny," he said, "you're a fellow with no nerves. I only wish I could be near enough to see you face Orping. I—I'm going to pray for you, Dan!"

He went down the hall and down the stairs with a pinched heart. He wanted to stay beside his friend. He could understand the whole thing perfectly. He was being sent out of harm's way, and then, when the great Jas Orping came, Dan Travis would face him. It would be a battle of giants! And he, Clancy Morgan, would be cowering in the shack of his friend!

Well, he certainly would be a fool if he tried to resist the will of Travis. He went to the stable, saddled his horse, and rode around to the front of the hotel. The clerk was on the veranda, with his hands in his hip pockets, chewing tobacco and rocking from heel to toe in time with the champing of the quid.

"Riding?" asked the clerk with a vague eye.

"I'm going out to the Travis place," said Clancy Mor-

gan. He had been permitted to say that much. Then he
added: "If anybody asks for me, say where I am."

The clerk said nothing. But he stopped his rocking from
heel to toe. He went to the edge of the veranda and stared
down the street after the disappearing rider. So Clancy
Morgan put the sandy hill between him and Tartartown,
and came to the shack of Dan Travis, where one half of
his destiny was to be fulfilled.

CHAPTER 11
Jasper Orping

THE SHACK WAS AS NEAT AS A PIN. TRAVIS HAD LEFT THE remains of a small fire smoking on the hearth. Although the heat was trifling, all the smoke went up the yawning chimney. That was like Travis. He would always be the fellow to build a fireplace that would draw.

Clancy Morgan examined the pots. There was a quantity of beans in one, steaming slowly over the fire. The sight of them, the porky smell of them, made him hungry. It was almost noon. He found some bread and put coffee and water in the coffeepot. Then he went into the shed at the end of the cabin to get more wood.

He was surprised at what he found there. A good bit of the hard, twisted roots of the mesquite lay in a corner. The other end of the shed was corded up with sawed lengths of fence posts. Some fence line must have been shifted recently, and Travis had brought in the discarded old posts.

It seemed odd to Morgan. For he remembered that when he had come to the cabin the other day, Travis said he'd been out digging mesquite roots. But here was wood of both kinds, the iron-strong, long-burning mesquite, ideal for keeping a pot simmering, and the quick-burning fence posts. Why had Travis been digging more roots?

Well, that was the way of Travis. He certainly wasn't short of wood, as he said, but perhaps had been short of a certain type of the roots. He was the sort of a fellow who knew all the fine points about everything.

With some of the light wood of the posts, Morgan built up the fire until the coffee boiled. Then he made a meal of beans and bread and black coffee. He was ashamed he could eat with such a good appetite. It was, he told himself, like consuming the body of his friend, who was waiting back there in the town to confront a mortal peril. Nevertheless, he ate and then smoked a cigarette.

Olivia had said that Dan Travis wanted to see him, Clancy, dead on the ground. Olivia had said that! Great-hearted Dan Travis, who was now facing death, with his perfect calm of demeanor.

Clancy could see him stepping forth into the street and waving a hand at Orping.

"Jasper," he would say, "I believe you're hunting for a friend of mine. I'm standing in that friend's shoes. Fill your hand!"

It would be something like that. The men of the range would never finish talking about it.

A horse loped over the hill from Tartartown and swung down the nearer slope; a horse taller than a mustang, reaching out with a ground-covering gallop. The man in the saddle sat canted forward a little, to accommodate himself to the speed of his mount. He had wide shoulders; his sombrero brim fanned straight up above his forehead.

There was something familiar about him. With every stride of the horse that sense of familiarity grew in the mind of Clancy Morgan. He stood up. But he did not know what worried him. It was simply that the figure of that rider was connected in the back of the mind of Morgan, with an unpleasant something that he could not specify.

He could see the foam on the neck of the horse, where the reins had chafed the sweat. He could see the fling of the forehoofs. The horse had the look of a thoroughbred; it had the sweep and winging ease of a thoroughbred's gallop.

Then a stroke of blind fear dimmed the eyes of Clancy Morgan. For he could make out the face of the rider, and he placed the resemblance now. It was a resemblance to Bill Orping—it was such a striking resemblance that it could be no other than Jasper Orping, who had ridden through the town without being checked by Dan Travis!

What had gone wrong? Had Orping failed to take the direct route to the town? If so, how had he guessed that his victim was at the Travis place? Who could have known, except the hotel clerk and a very few others?

A sort of madness came over Clancy Morgan. He wanted to shout that there was a mistake. But it was too late for such shouting. It was too late to do anything, unless he chose to run back inside the house—and then be shot, through a window or a crack in the door like a rat in its hole.

No, to go back inside seemed like going back into a coffin.

He saw the rider pull up suddenly and swing to the ground. He was taller than Bill Orping. His legs were not so bowed. But it was certainly a brotherly resemblance. Ah, if Dan Travis had only been there!

Jasper Orping walked straight on. He was hardly ten paces away when he halted.

"Fellow," he said, "are you the two-legged rat that goes by the name of Clancy Morgan?"

"Orping," shouted Clancy, "I didn't kill Bill!"

"You lie!" said Orping, and went for his gun.

It seemed to Clancy Morgan that bullets were already striking him, while he tugged out his own Colt.

The lightning flash in the hand of Orping exploded. The hat left the head of Clancy Morgan. The sun blinded his eyes. Into the blaze of light he aimed. Another bullet stung his ear like a wasp. Then he fired.

Jasper Orping spun around and toppled with his back to the leveled gun.

Chapter 12
The Second Chance

ORPING TRIED TO ROLL OVER ON HIS OTHER SIDE, TO continue shooting, but something hindered him. Clancy Morgan walked up softly, so that his gun held steadily on the target.

"If you try to shoot again, I'll kill you, Orping," he said. "I've got you covered."

"High and to the right!" groaned Orping. "I told the jackass it was shooting high and to the right. Oh, I'm a fool!"

He sat up. The gun that had fallen from his hand lay almost buried in dust. Morgan knelt behind him and laid the muzzle of that gun against the back of Orping's thick neck.

"Why don't you shoot?" said Orping. "You're the boy who loves to get 'em from behind, you dirty killer, you!"

"Take it easy," said Clancy, "I didn't shoot *you* from behind. And I'll tell you this—I never aimed a gun at Bill. Someday you'll find out. Hold still while I get your hardware."

79

There were three guns in all, and a formidable knife. Clancy took them and stood up.

"Where is it?" he asked.

"Aw, you got me through the left leg," snarled Jarper Orping. "Why don't you finish the job? I'm damned if I want to live after a half-baked kid puts me down like this."

The dazzle was not of sun in the eyes of Clancy Morgan now, but of a marvel which had been accomplished. He could not say how he felt, except numb. He had no sense of triumph. "High and to the right" that Colt of Orping's had certainly carried, or else Clancy would have been twice dead before he pulled the trigger of his own weapon.

He put his hands under the pits of Orping's shoulders and lifted him to his feet.

"A filthy brat—to roll *me*!" groaned Orping.

"Put your left arm across my shoulders." Clancy Morgan gripped the iron-hard body of Orping with his own right arm, and so helped him into the cabin and onto the bunk of Dan Travis.

What would Travis think when he found the great enemy subdued, and in his own house?

"A brat!" moaned Jas Orping. "A murdering brat! How old are you?"

"Twenty-two," said Clancy, cutting away the trouser leg from the wound of Orping.

"Twenty-two," sighed Orping.

He lay back, his hands folded under his head. His broad, savage face worked spasmodically, not with pain, but with his mental torment of shame.

"I know it was only luck," said Clancy. "I'm not proud of myself."

The lip of Orping lifted away from his yellow teeth. He said nothing. And Clancy bathed the wound, stopped the blood with dust, and wound a bandage around the hurt.

"Does it feel better?" he asked.

Orping said nothing. After his first outburst, he seemed

to hate speech as much as he hated Clancy Morgan. But with his vicious eyes he followed the youngster around the hut.

He accepted a tin cup of coffee and drank it off at two swallows. He accepted a cigarette, also, and, smoked it half down before he said:

"And now what? One murder's enough, eh? You won't put me out of my misery? You'll wait for the sheriff to get me, eh?"

"I don't want to harm you, Orping," said Clancy Morgan. "You came at me like a tiger. I had to shoot, and I was lucky. That's all."

"He's only a kid, and he's put both the Orpings down! He's only a kid!" groaned Orping.

Hoofbeats came up the trail. Clancy yearned to go to the door to see who might be coming, but dared not leave his formidable prisoner. The man lay like a savage beast, his powerful body stirring now and then, and his mouth working with rage. Given two seconds, he would get to his guns, even though he had to drag one useless leg; and, once armed, he could be trusted not to miss a second opportunity.

The rider coming up the trail halted at the cabin; the door was kicked open, and there appeared first a hand and a leveled gun, and then the grim face of Dan Travis.

"He got through, Dan," said Clancy Morgan modestly, "but luck stopped him. He could have planted me twice, but his gun was out of kilter. Here's Orping!"

Travis said nothing by way of answer. He made no excuse for not stopping his man in town. Instead, he stalked over to the bunk and stared down at Jas Orping.

"How are you, Jas," he asked quietly.

"Travis," said Orping, "do you hold with this murdering rat of a kid? Is that where you stand?"

Still Travis said nothing. He stepped back, looked around the room, and finally included Clancy Morgan with his glance. Perhaps it was the fury of shame and of disappointment that silenced him—shame and rage because he had not managed to block this gunman on the way through Tartartown.

"What did you use on him?" asked Travis suddenly.

"The old gun you gave me a year ago, Danny," said Morgan.

"Let me see it," demanded Travis.

"Here you are."

He passed it over. Travis broke it open and took out the shells.

"You got him with one slug," he muttered.

"My gun was carrying high and to the right," said Orping. "I guessed it with the first shot, but still I didn't correct it enough. Blast me for a fool! I'd sighted it myself just yesterday but something must of gotten out of kilter during my ride. And he nailed me through the leg. That sneak—he stood there and nailed me through the leg! I ain't a man no more. I'm a dirty Siwash. I'll take water from a Chinaman—and every fool of a kid knocks me over the first try!"

He beat his great brown hands against his face.

"Take it easy," said Travis, slipping the cartridges back into Morgan's gun. "maybe you'll have another chance."

"Me? Another chance at what?" demanded Orping.

"At him," said Travis.

"Yeah? And how does that come about?"

"Could you stand on that leg?" said Travis.

"I could hop a mile on it," said Orping. "What's that to you?"

"You won't have to hop a mile," answered Travis. "You'll only have to hop outside this cabin. That's all. Can you do that?"

"Of course I can. What for?"

"For your second chance at Morgan," said Travis. "Clancy, help him off that bunk!"

''Why, Danny,'' said Morgan, wondering, ''what's the matter?''

''You are a rat!'' snarled Dan Travis. ''You've shot his brother through the back, and now Orping is going to have a chance to make you stand up like a man and shoot straight if you can!''

The horror of the betrayal came like a slow dawn over the brain of Clancy Morgan. ''Danny!'' he said. ''You don't mean it?''

''You dog!'' said Travis. ''I've always hated your guts! Your pretty face that the girls like so well—maybe Orping can change the look of it—and if he doesn't, *I will*!''

''You want to see me,'' said Morgan brokenly, incredulously, ''dead at your feet!''

''I do!'' shouted Travis, his voice suddenly filling the room. ''And that's where I'll see you! You fool! I've used you, and now I'm through with you! Help him off that bunk!''

''She told me,'' said Clancy Morgan, his brain working slowly forward. ''She said that's what you wanted—to see me dead at your feet!''

''Who told you?'' demanded Travis.

''She—Olivia.''

''Did she guess that?'' snarled Travis. ''Aye, but I'll lay your ghost, and I'll change her mind. I'll change it by the way I mourn over you. Handsome Clancy Morgan, eh? I stood and watched 'em, ready to hang you, and I laughed, Morgan.

''But the devil taught you the way out of that tangle, curse you. Now let the devil teach you the way out of this! Help Jasper off the bunk and outside the house. I'll see you fight him first. And if he doesn't finish you, I'll do the job. I'll make a pattern of Handsome Clancy's face for him!''

Morgan, with fumbling hands, and sinking heart, his head whirling, helped Orping to his feet.

"I'll never forget this, Danny," said Orping. "You won't need to finish nothing! I'll handle him. And I'll be a friend to you for the rest of your days, Travis. There's something in you, after all. Bill seemed to hate you. But there's something in you I like. There's no soft pulp about you. You know how to hate an enemy, and that means you know how to love a friend."

"Orping," said Dan Travis, "I'll tell you this—that friendship is a sacred thing to me—the most sacred thing in the world!"

"I believe you," said Orping. "Let's get out outdoors. I'll blow his face off his skull, man. I'll pulverize him! But first we'd better make him tell us what he did with the money!"

Clancy Morgan was supporting the brutal body of Orping before him, and Orping hopped toward the door of the shack.

"What money?" asked Travis blankly.

"Why, Bill had quite a roll on him. He must 'a had, because I know he made a big clean-up in a poker game not long ago. What became of the money?"

"We'll find out!" said Travis grimly.

A thought had driven home like a spur into Morgan. He swayed Orping so that the ruffian staggered.

"Steady!" said Clancy Morgan, lurching against the wall. And as he lurched, he struck back-handed at the gun in the hand of Travis.

The bullet hurled under the arm of Clancy and into the 'dobe wall.

Then Clancy Morgan, striking with all his desperate might, lodged the ridge of his hard knuckles on the long, projecting chin of Travis. Travis dropped to his knees, and Clancy Morgan tore the gun out of his nerveless hand.

CHAPTER 13
Hypocrite's End

Clancy tied Travis's left arm to the right arm of Orping. Together he drove them out of the house, into the blinding brightness of the sun; and still Travis cursed him with a ferocity that knew no fear of death.

"The whole soul of me's been turning sour because I've had to smile at you this long time," said Travis. "But it was only because you were the world to the girl, that I held myself in. I held myself in. Handsome Clancy! I tell you, I regret nothing, except that they didn't hang up Handsome Clancy by the throat. Where you taking us?"

"When I saw you yesterday morning," said Clancy Morgan, his face as rigid as white iron, "you had a shovel in your hand. Go get that shovel."

"What the devil for?" demanded Travis.

"To dig more of the same mesquite roots you were digging then," said Clancy.

So he forced the wavering, unsteady couple forward through the sand until the shovel was found. He drove them still farther, until in the middle of a dense mass of mesquite, they reached a place where the surface crust of the sand had been newly disturbed.

"Dig there!" he cried.

"Damn you," said Travis. "I won't lift a hand!"

"I'll burn some new ideas into you if you don't," answered Clancy Morgan. "I want to keep my hands off you, Travis, but if I have a good excuse, I'll flay the hide off the worst murdering hypocrite in the world. Dig there, and dig hard!"

He set him free from the wounded man, and in three brief minutes Travis turned up a bit of tarpaulin, and in that tarpaulin was a roll of greenbacks.

"There's the money," said Clancy Morgan. "And there's the man who shot your brother in the back, Orping, and then let me take the blame for it. There's the man who says friendship is sacred. He murdered Bill Orping after he'd talked him into turning his back. He took Bill's money and buried it out here, and if there's a law in the land, he'll hang for it—he and his perfect friendship!"

Orping, with a wild cry, snatched the shovel and tried to brain big Dan Travis with it, but Morgan stopped his hand.

Travis himself, before the insane fury of Jasper Orping, whitened, and began to shake. He seemed barely to have strength to obey the guns in the hand of Morgan and help the wounded man back to the house.

"If you stay here," said Morgan, "you'll go to jail, you say, Orping. And maybe you deserve to be in jail. But the way I see you, you're a fellow who tried to do the right thing by your brother. Aye, friendship might be a sacred thing to you! Anyway, there's the money your brother had. Take it. Take your horse, too. It will hurt to ride with that leg, but it can't be helped. You'll do one thing for me when you're safe with your friends. Write me a letter and put in it everything you saw and heard today between me and Travis. The law may want to know."

"The law may take him," said Orping grimly. "And the law had better make an end of him, I can tell you that! But you, Morgan, I'll remember you. The whole world is goin' to remember you, too, because this traitor here is black enough to make you shine whiter than snow!"

Clancy Morgan never saw Orping again. He took Dan Travis—a snarling, beastlike Travis—into the town, and saw the jail close over him. Then happiness settled down with a smile over the house of Harry Gregor.

There was still a month before the wedding. It was nearly at the end of that time before Clancy Morgan could gather his courage to ask Olivia what had given her insight into the hatred which Travis felt for him to such a consummate degree.

"Because he came to me and talked about you," said the girl. "He knew I loved to hear about you. I think he used to make up all sorts of stories to show how intimate you two were. And then, one day, when I was laughing and happy, I saw his face, and it was frozen into a horrible mask of hate—hate of you, Clancy! I knew it then. But you loved him so much I never dared to speak until that last day."

"I never loved him," said Clancy Morgan bitterly. "I only loved the lie that he was making himself appear when I was around. I was a fool, Olivia. I'll never trust my judgment about people again."

"No," said the girl. "You can trust your judgment of people well enough. Think how well you see through me, Clancy, and how well you weigh and measure me! But, seriously, I don't think the devil walks the earth in more than one man at a time; and the devil was in poor Dan Travis."

" 'Poor Dan Travis'?" echoed Clancy Morgan. "Aye," he added, "I know what you mean. If he had been honest, if he had been what he seemed, he would have been better than a king. But the devil was walking in him all the time.''

CARCAJOU'S
TRAIL

CHAPTER 1
Back-Throw

Two boats were just in from Juneau, and Dyea was filled with excited men and howling dogs. Over in Chilkoot Pass, where misery and folly crowded in together, men were laboring, but no one between the mountains and the sea could realize the importance of the man who stood at Steuermann's bar in Dyea. This man was John Banner. That name never became famous in the North, but ask any of the old-timers if they ever have heard of a fellow nicknamed "Carcajou."

Carcajou is French Canadian for wolverene, and it is worth while knowing something about the animal before you try to comprehend the man.

The wolverene is the largest weasel, as a matter of fact, but it looks like a little humpbacked caricature of a bear. Some of the Indians call it "skunk bear."

It has short legs and a long, weasel body. It has claws with which it can chisel through yards of frozen ground to get at a buried cache which the keenest sense of smell in all the world has enabled it to locate. It has the biting power of a wolf and the tenacity of a bulldog. It is stronger, pound for pound, than any animal in the world.

A one-hundred-and-twenty-pound timber wolf simply turns aside and gives up the trail when it sees the wolverene come padding toward it; for it knows that the smaller animal will not budge from the path, and that it is better to tamper with dynamite than with the compressed ferocity of this beast.

The strength of the wolverene is explained by the fact that there is not a straight line in it. Legs, back, neck, body, all are curves that loop into one another and give continual reenforcement. But the strength of spirit is greater than the strength of flesh. The Indians say that the soul of the carcajou is the soul of Satan.

At any rate, it combines the terrible blood lust of the weasel with the patience of a grizzly bear. It is the only one of the weasel family distinguished for intelligence, and it seems as though the wits of the entire species are concentrated in that one small brain, for trappers will tell you that nothing that lives in the wilderness compares with the carcajou for diabolical cleverness.

There are stories about old and cunning trappers with many years of experience who have been driven from fine trapping grounds by the ferocious cunning of the wolverene, which will follow the trap lines, avoiding all poisoned bait, and ruin the pelts of the trapped creatures which it does not devour. It has been known to work for long days, carefully prying and tugging, trying one leverage after another, until it has found a way into a ponderously built log cache. Thus, men have died when, at the end of the long winter marches, they have found the cache gone.

This is not a full portrait of the carcajou. It is only a sketch, and if you wish to get even an inkling of the true nature of the beast, you must go far north and abandon yourself for many a long winter evening to talk of the

French Canadian trappers, who will tell you tales in which the carcajou gradually ceases to be animal, and passes into that legendary realm between flesh and fancy, where only the werewolf exists.

Bearing all of these things in mind, look now behind the doors of Steuermann's through the mist of steam and smoke at John Banner, who is to receive his new baptism of blood and to be renamed Carcajou before this day is an hour older.

At first sight there is nothing unusual about him. He is simply a fellow of middle height, looking rather plump, and, on the whole, lethargic. You will guess his weight at a hundred and sixty, and thereby you will make your first mistake, because there are twenty extra pounds under the loose clothes. Look again to note the depth and roundness of the barrel of the man.

Gradually you see that here is a man composed of nothing but curves, that run, looping and subtly reenforcing one another. The shoulders slope into arms big at the top and tapering down to a perfectly round wrist. The hand that holds the glass of whisky on the edge of the bar is daintily and delicately made. Perhaps the length of the thumb is rather unusual.

Still, look as closely as you can, there is nothing very unusual about him, except that you begin to feel that perhaps what seems plumpness is not fat at all. At least, the line of the cheek bone and the jaw is clear cut and firm enough. Perhaps under the clothes the body of the man is like India rubber, firm and resilient.

So much for John Banner at this moment. More is to come. In the meantime, there were other people in that barroom worthy of attention. Just inside the door, pushing back the furred hood from his face, was Bill Roads, a huge, rawboned, powerful man. He looked over the crowd with the air of one who hopes to find a face. When his glance rested on the form of John Banner, it was plain that he had arrived at the object of his quest; his face contorted, and a light flared in his eyes. He started weaving through the crowd, with his gaze fixed upon the goal, and one hand dropped into the deep pocket of his coat.

Down the bar, not far from Banner, stood a pair of big French Canadians, smiling men, contented with themselves. They had made one fortune "inside," and they were going after another. Wise in the ways of the wilderness, their strength was more than doubled, because they were devoted friends, each ready to guard the back of the other against every danger, and ever on the watch to give needed help.

Beyond the French Canadians there was an odd group of three, a group whose importance was to appear later. Jimmy Slade was there, and Charley Horn, their ruffian natures clearly appearing in their faces, and between them was that good old man, Tom Painter—"Old Tom" to most men.

He was not so very old, either; not more, say, than fifty-nine or sixty, but men of that age are old for the Far North. There was about his face an air of gentle resignation, as of one who has endured much pain and prepares to endure yet more before the end will come. The bartender, after filling a glass, pushed it across the bar and inside the grasp of the waiting hand of Old Tom. Then the veteran looked up with a smile, and the eyes were empty, totally darkened. Even a child could tell that he was blind.

Steuermann stared hard at him. "Are you going inside, Old Tom?" he asked.

"Going back inside once more, the last time, Steuermann," said Old Tom.

"Along with these here friends of yours?" asked the bartender.

"You ain't met 'em yet, I guess," said Old Tom.

"Here's Charley Horn on my right and Jim Slade on my left. Shake hands with Steuermann, boys, will you?"

They extended their hands with muttered words of greeting. Their eyes, keen and suspicious, probed at the mind of Steuermann, as though wondering how far he might suspect them of dark deeds. He, however, had looked at them before, and did not feel it was necessary to look again. Dark deeds were exactly what the pair seemed equipped for.

Worse faces than these had been turned toward the Chilkoot. There was nothing strange about that. Only, why were they the companions of a blind man?

That was a question worth an answer!

"You'll find the trail sort of rough, won't you, Tom?" asked Steuermann.

"I can walk pretty good with a stick to feel the way," answered Old Tom. "Besides, we've got a good outfit, and I guess I'll have to ride a mighty big part of the way."

"A long way, eh?" asked Steuermann.

"All ways are long up this far north, ain't they?" answered Jimmy Slade, cutting sharply in.

"Oh, any way will be a pretty long way for me, Steuermann," said Old Tom.

The bartender just shrugged his shoulders. It had not been his intention to ask prying questions. It was merely that pity and interest bubbled up in him as he saw the helpless veteran and the two roughnecks who were his escort.

This conversation took place while big Bill Roads worked his way in from the door toward his man. He did not come up from the side, but from behind, where Banner stood at the bar with a glass of whisky poised in his hand.

He was close behind his quarry when the men on the right and left of him pressed suddenly back; for they saw that Roads had drawn a gun and at the same instant shouted: "Hands up, Banner, or take it in the back!"

Banner moved to throw up his hands, but as the right hand rose above his shoulder it flung the whisky out of the glass straight behind him.

Perhaps it was partly fortune; perhaps in greater part it was uncanny skill in locating the speaker by the mere sound of his voice. But certainly, a few drops of the stinging liquor splashed into the eyes of Roads.

He fired twice. The two bullets smashed through the mirror behind the bar, the pride of Steuermann, and left two small holes, surrounded by the white of powdered glass, from which the cracks extended outward in long, wavering lines.

The second shot was the last that Roads could fire, for Banner was in at him by that time. He did not strike with his fists, but he caught hold of big Roads with his hands, and as though the touch were molten lead, Roads yelled with pain and fear for help. Then he went down.

There was something grisly about the sudden paralysis that seized on Roads. It was as though the spider had been stung by the poison of the smaller wasp, as if an electric shock had numbed all of the vital nerve centers. He still writhed and struggled, but blindly, helplessly, with rapidly decreasing strength.

Then the bystanders saw, with horror, what was happening, as Roads suddenly stopped struggling and began to scream. There were no words, no appeals for help, but simply terrible shrieking. Banner had his elbows on the shoulders of the fallen man, and with his hands interlocked under the chin of Roads, was forcing back his head farther and farther to break his neck.

CHAPTER 2
Corded Strength

THEY LUNGED FOR BANNER THEN. THEY LAID ON HIM powerful hands, only to find that their fingers, under his clothes, impinged on quivering masses of corded strength on which they could get no hold.

The French Canadians were among the first to try to pry the killer from his victim. One of them, after a mighty effort, muttered through his teeth to his friend: "Carcajou!"

That was how the nickname originated—"Carcajou!" And the hoarse screams of the victim began to be throttled by the distance to which his head had been forced back. The windpipe was closing. The spinal column itself would snap and shatter presently.

Charley Horn was among those present, bending over the twisting, struggling men, his hands on his knees. He was laughing under his breath, a very horrible sound to those who heard it. But now he reached down and struck with the edge of his hand across the top of the neck of Banner.

It was enough. For half a second the killer was paralyzed, and in that moment he was torn from the victim.

He stood back by the bar, looking down at big Roads. His face was utterly immobile, except that there was a slight cut in his upper lip, and the red tip of his tongue was touching the wound thoughtfully, tasting his own blood.

"What were you trying to do—murder a man?" shouted Steuermann, shaking his fist under the nose of Banner. "A carcajou is what you are! A regular murdering wolverene!"

The Carcajou lifted his glance and stared at Steuermann. It was only a glance, but it made Steuermann snatch out a revolver from beneath the bar.

The Carcajou laid his left hand on the edge of the bar.

"I'd put that gun down if I were you," said he.

It was the first time he had spoken, and there was such a passionless calm in his voice that those who heard could not believe their ears. Steuermann was a brave man, as he'd proved over and over again, but he put down the gun.

People remembered it afterward, and not a man who was present blamed him for taking water at that particular moment, and from that particular man.

The Carcajou left the saloon, stepping lightly, unconcernedly, through the crowd, asking the pardon of those he shouldered against, and always speaking in that same impassive voice which might have seemed perfectly gentle had not the others seen what he had done.

But now he was gone, and poor Bill Roads was stretched on a table near the stove, gasping for breath.

They forgot they had seen him try to shoot a man from behind. In fact, it did not seem to be a man, but a monster superhumanly evil. Besides, as they opened his coat to give him air, they saw the badge of a Federal officer of the law. They poured a stiff drink of whisky down his throat. His head was pillowed on a rolled-up coat.

"How is it?" said Steuermann, who'd taken charge.

"I don't know. My neck may be broken. I heard the bones snapping, I thought!"

He closed his eyes and gasped again. Then, his eyes still closed, he muttered: "I thought I had him at last. Ten thousand miles, and I thought I had him at last!"

One who'd been a doctor in quieter days of his life took charge of the injured man, fingered the back of Road's neck, moved his head up and down.

"The neck isn't broken," he said. "You'll be all right; but you need to be put to bed. You've had a shock, man, and that's why your temperature came up so fast! Get him into a bed quick, some of you boys!"

"Get Banner, first," pleaded Bill Roads. "Get Banner, and let me go hang. I don't care what happens to me. I only care that he's caught."

"We'll attend to him later," said Steuermann. "We ain't got time to gather him in just now. Take it easy, man. Take it easy. Don't go and burn yourself up. What kind of a crook is this here Banner, this here Carcajou?"

"Crook? He's more than a crook. He's a fiend. He's a jungle cat. He came out of the New York slums. There's nothing but Satan in him. Get him dead or alive. There's a reward. I don't want any share. There's ten thousand dollars!"

Ten thousand dollars!

It was a fortune. With it a man could go back to civilization without ever enduring the strain and daring the dangers of the terrible venture into the inside. He would have his stake ready-made. Yet not a man left the saloon on the blood trail.

To be sure, Horn looked at Jimmy Slade, but Slade muttered: "Ten thousand dollars ain't enough to buy the amount of prussic acid you'd need to bump off that bird. Bullets, they wouldn't be no good. They'd just bounce off the surface, is all!"

The blind man asked no questions, but he waited with a troubled face, looking down always.

"Just a bird that hopped in here and done a gun play and got flopped on his back for his trouble," said Charley Horn. "That's all, Old Tom. There wa'n't no real trouble at all. Not the killing kind, but the gent who done the shooting pretty near got his neck broke."

He chuckled a little. A hard man was Charley Horn; just a trifle harder than Jimmy Slade, though there wasn't much to choose between.

"Too bad, too bad!" said Old Tom. "When folks get this far north they seem to think they've left kindness and decency behind 'em—sometimes. And that's too bad, too!"

His two evil-faced companions glanced askance at one another. Somebody was saying to Bill Roads: "What's this gent done? This Carcajou?"

"Banner? Carcajou? What does Carcajou mean?"

"A weasel with the meanness of a weasel, the brain of a grizzly, and the most of a bear's strength, too."

"You've found the right name for him, then," said Roads. "But talking about him is no good. I'd have to spend days telling you what he's done. I'd have to tell you how I've done nothing but follow him for two years; and follow him I still will, working for the government or working for myself. I'll crawl on my hands around the whole world, but finally I'll split his skull with a bullet, or run a knife through his heart! He's got to die!"

He was panting as he spoke these last words. Then a spasm of pain got him once more, and he groaned.

The others listened to him with a singular respect. A two-year-old blood trail is very interesting indeed. Yet the thought of the ten thousand dollars' reward did not induce a single man there to leave the saloon and track down the enemy of society.

The trouble was that they had seen too much and too

intimately the dealings of John Banner in that same room. They did not want to find themselves flattened on the ground with the hands of the monster on their throats.

"It's a funny thing," said Steuermann, shaking his head, though "funny" was not really the word he wanted. "It's a funny thing he didn't take a shorter way of murdering you, man, when he had you spread out like that!"

"What's killing more or less to him?" asked the officer of the law. "What does it matter to a demon like Banner? Not a thing! Killing, bit by bit, with his hands, that's what would please him. Three mortal times he could have killed me on this trail, and three times he's refused to shoot—he's tried to get at me with his hands every time."

They listened with horror. There was hardly a man in that room with delicate sensibilities. But what they heard was sufficient to make them sick.

Afterwards, if fifty thousand dollars had been offered instead of ten, it would not have been enough to get any man, or any four men, out of that room on the trail of the Carcajou.

Steuermann found, at this point, a chance to draw Jimmy Slade to one side.

Ordinarily he would not have dreamed of talking as he was about to talk now. But enough had happened to excite him highly, and his tongue broke loose from the usually severely imposed restraints.

"Slade," he said, "I've got to ask you a question. Where do you intend to go with Old Tom?"

Slade looked boldly and contemptuously into the eyes of the bartender. "Ask me again another way," he said. "I don't understand that kind of language."

Steuermann darkened and drew back a little.

"All right," he said. "Only, brother, I wanta tell you one thing."

"Tell it soft and low, then," said Slade, growing uglier every moment.

101

"I'll tell you this. Old Tom ain't a stranger up here."

"No?"

"No, he's not a stranger. And if he goes in blind with you and your side-kicker, there's gonna be a whole lot of us anxious to see him come out again."

Slade stepped closer. "Now, whacha mean by that?" he demanded savagely.

"You know what I mean," said Steuermann without flinching. "I've told you what I mean, and I guess you understand the language."

"Say it over once more, brother," said Slade through his teeth.

"I'll say it over," answered the bartender. "We'll be looking to see you and Horn come out with Old Tom still alongside of you."

"And where else would he be?" demanded Slade.

"Dead of frostbite, somewhere inside," said Steuermann, and turned back behind his bar.

CHAPTER 3
The Wager

WHEN THE NEWLY NAMED CARCAJOU STEPPED OUTSIDE the saloon, he stood for a moment and breathed in the air, pure, free from smoke—free, it also seemed to him, even from the language of man.

Within the doors he could hear the murmur of voices which had been loosed the moment he left the room, but he regarded this not at all, except as a sign of his freedom.

Mankind meant nothing to the Carcajou, except in so far as the race furnished for him interesting enemies. Now and then the contest was close; now and again the fight was hard; but the victory was always his.

There might be, somewhere on the planet, men swifter, stronger, fiercer, more cunning than he; but he never had met such a one. Having gone unconquered all of his days, he expected to remain so to the end.

As for friends, he never had known one, male or female, who valued him as much as they valued the price on his head. That price was of long standing, from the time he was fifteen, in fact. Doubtless the price would not have been placed had his age been known. At fifteen he looked twenty, at least. At twenty-five he looked still hardly more than twenty. Ten years of breaking and evading the law had not aged him.

The reason he paused now was not because he did not know where to go. It was simply that he was hesitating, wondering whether he really wished that famous man of the law, Bill Roads, dead or alive. He could have killed Bill easily enough. But if Bill were off the trail, what would remain to make things really interesting for him? Who would be able to make him sleep like a wolf, with one eye open? Who would be able to make him keep constantly on the alert, waiting and peering about for danger?

Bill Roads was, on the whole, the most formidable enemy he'd ever known. Four times Roads had come in close contact with him. Four times he'd defeated the enemy. This day he had wished to kill the man, but on the whole, he was rather glad he hadn't.

One does not wish to subtract from life all of its spice! When he reached this conclusion he nodded slightly and set off down the street.

It was snowing, large crisp flakes that came down in wavering strokes of dimness before his eyes. Where they touched his face they did not seem very cold. There was a pleasant sound of them underfoot. The air was not yet iced. It was rather moist and still. And straight down the street he could see still the leaden waters of the sea.

On the whole he was content. Actual happiness he never knew, except when he was cracking a safe, say, or at grips with a foeman. But now he was fairly well pleased with himself. He had discovered that life in the States was growing a little too warm for him. He might, it was true, avoid the law for another few months, but he knew there were too many posters about him here and there. And ten thousand dollars is a large enough sum of money to put brains in the most stupid and courage in the cowardly. He had evaded destruction a hundred times, to be sure, but in the end the luck would turn against him and he would go down. Small comfort to him if he lay one day gasping on his back, grasping at the mud with his mighty hands, if he knew that the bullet that laid him low had been fired by a tyro, whom chance had favored.

So he determined to leave the states and make his way toward the great white North.

He intended to go inland where he would be lost among the shifting crowds of miners for perhaps a year. When he came out again, no doubt the memory of him would be slightly more dim in the minds of the police. After that he could take a trip around the world and let his repute become still less familiar. When he returned to New York— well, then the old world would not know him, and he would begin the nefarious practices which he loved once more.

This was his general plan of campaign. This was his strategy. As for tactics, he was prepared to deal with each situation as it arose. He was not one to worry about the future. As he had dealt with Bill Roads in the saloon, so he had dealt with other enemies from time to time, and so he would deal with them again in the future.

It must not be thought that there was a blind confidence in the Carcajou. He seriously had waited, all the days of his life, to find another man superior to himself in power, in speed and cruelly quick decision. He did not pray to encounter such a dreadful foe, but he yearned for the meeting as a child may yearn to have a younger brother born.

Striding down the street, he passed a gap between the buildings on his left and heard the shoutings of a small crowd, the snarling of a dog, the curses of a man. It was not a pretty scene.

A big crate stood open in the space between two buildings, and a dog on a long chain had been let out of the crate. Just beyond the length of chain stood a man with a club, and as the dog rushed at him, he beat the beast to the ground again and again.

"You'll never break that dog that way," said the Carcajou to himself.

He canted his head to one side as he stood and watched. Perhaps there was enough of the animal in him to make him sympathize. Now, at least, he thought that he understood in a flash the entire workings of the brain of the dog.

It was a monster Husky, its blood enriched with many crossings of the timber wolf, but of a size the wolf never attains. What could the other strain or strains be?

It was a frightful mongrel. That much was clear. It had the mousy, immense head of an Irish wolfhound. It had also the stature of that terrific beast. But there was the coat of a wolf; and the weight in the shoulders and in the quarters was more than an Irish wolfhound would ever be likely to show. Carcajou would not venture to guess lightly at the total burden of this frightful thing—two hundred pounds, perhaps, or even more.

As it lay flat on the ground, it seemed less. When it rose into the air at the dog breaker it seemed as huge as a bear. Now the monster got up from the mud and snow, shook himself, and crouched, without charging. His head was bleeding. No matter whether he charged high or low, the club always met him, swinging in that expert hand. Always the exactly timed blow crashed down upon his head.

So he waited, now, panting with fury rather than with effort, and lolling out his long red tongue, he looked at the dog breaker with eyes redder still. The latter shouted with angry triumph and shook his left fist, cursing.

"Come on, you! I've got plenty more of the same kind left!"

It was plain from the triumph in his tone that he dreaded this encounter.

The Carcajou stepped up and said: "You'll never break him that way."

The dog breaker stepped back out of range of the monster and turned furiously on this mere human antagonist. The brute in him mantled in his face. "You'll tell me how to break dogs, will you?"

"I could tell you a point or two," said the Carcajou in that same tone of misleading gentleness. In fact, his voice was never raised. He never had shouted out loud in all his life, since a certain dreadful moment in his childhood.

"You could tell me a point or two, could you, you slab-faced piece of fish, you flounder-faced piece of putty, you!" shouted the dog breaker.

The Carcajou stepped closer, and with a swift, inescapable movement of his left hand, caught the club arm of the other above the wrist.

The dog breaker looked down. The club fell from his paralyzed hand. The fury left his face. White wonder took its place.

"Well," he muttered. "What would you do with him?"

"That's a dog for a dog team, isn't it?" asked the Carcajou.

"That ain't a dog. That's a dog team," said the breaker. "That's a man-killer, too."

"Oh, is he?"

"He's worse than killed Larry Patrick last week. Larry ain't gonna be no more than sewed-up chunks of a man the rest of his days." Then he added: "What would you do with him, mister?"

"You've got to come to grips with him sooner or later. There's a brain behind those red eyes. You might teach him to be afraid of a club, but one day he'll catch you when you have no club in your hand."

"And then cut your throat, you mean?"

"Yes, unless he's been taught that your empty hands are better than his teeth."

"Empty hands!" repeated the dog breaker.

Other people in the crowd joined in his derisive laughter.

"Back up, stranger," said one man, "and let this here show go on! Back up, will you?"

The Carcajou looked on the unknown and smiled faintly. There was a certain richness of harvest, he found, in this land of the great white north. Wherever one turned there were reckless men, and a harvest of great danger. Gun or knife or hand, or all three, were ever ready to break out into action.

However, he merely said: "For a bet, I'd try my hand with that dog; my bare hands, I mean."

The stranger who had invited him to back up, cried instantly: "I've got five pounds of gold dust in this poke. Is that enough to make a bet for you?"

"That's about fifteen or sixteen hundred dollars, isn't it?" said the Carcajou. "All right. That will do."

Taking out his wallet, he began to count the sum requisite for the wager. The others fell silent.

CHAPTER 4
The Taming

"UNCHAIN THAT DOG," SAID THE CARCAJOU TO THE DOG breaker.

"I'll have to knock him cold before I can unchain him," said the breaker. "Besides, I wouldn't unchain him. I wouldn't turn loose that big streak of murder inside this town. If you wanta give him room, just walk into the circle he can run in, brother. That'll be about all."

"All right," said the Carcajou.

And he walked straight up to the dog.

It was an amazing thing to those who watched it. There had been excitement enough every time the great brute charged the man with the club. Now it brought each heart up into the throat to see one with empty hands go straight up to the monster and lay a hand on that bleeding head.

The dog crouched, snarling, but the green and red gleaming was out of its eyes, or very dim, at least.

The Carcajou talked straight down at him, his voice calm and gentle, as always, and as always, just a suggestion of iron clanking on iron somewhere in the sound.

They heard what he said, and remembered it.

"You're not such a bad one. You only think you're bad," said Carcajou to the dog. "You've had a fool slamming you over the head. But you'd rather wag your tail and be friends, if you could find the right man. I'm going to be the right man for you, boy. You can trust me."

The dog snarled, but there was a whine mingling with the snarl. The breaker yelled suddenly in rage and surprise: "He's a hypnotizer! That's what he is!"

At that shout, coming so suddenly, the great beast shot out his long neck and dragon's head to seize the Carcajou by the arm. The fangs slashed through the sleeve, cut the skin, but that was all. The Carcajou caught him by the throat and flung him to the ground.

He looked a little, puny thing, struggling with the huge brute, and he was flung here and there by the mighty struggles of the dog. The claws of the beast tore the heavy furs of the Carcajou to fragments and gouged his body. Blood dribbled on the snow, the blood of the Carcajou.

Then the dog made one great, last, convulsive motion and lay still, throttled to the verge of death, with his tongue hanging out of his mouth sidewise like a stream of purple-red blood.

The men who stood around had stopped shouting and jumping about in their excitement. They merely drew together and stared. With every fling from side to side of those dragonlike, gaping jaws, they expected to see the arms or the body of the man gashed to the bone. But though the strength of the brute was like that of a horse, it was securely held.

The Carcajou rose to his knees, patted the head of his victim, took a handful of snow and rubbed off the tongue, still hanging from the jaws, and patted the neck and back of the animal.

"What do you call the name of this little pet?" asked the Carcajou of the dog breaker.

The latter answered in newly humble tones: "He ain't

got any name. Slaughter would be about right for him, I reckon!''

"Sure it would," said the Carcajou.

He rose to his feet. Slaughter sprang up suddenly and stood on wavering legs, eyes still thrusting from its head, lungs heaving desperately. The Carcajou laid his hand a second time on the head of the great brute.

"Now we've been introduced, we can be good friends," he said.

"You better try sooner to be friendly with a pack of wild wolves," said the dog breaker. "That's what he is. A wild wolf is what he is, and he was runnin' wild when he was trapped."

"You mean," said the Carcajou, "that he was running with a wolf pack?"

"Yes, and the leader of it," said the breaker.

"Then he's worth having," said the Carcajou.

He reached out and took the canvas sack of gold dust from the hand of the silent, gloomy man who'd made and lost the bet. "What's the price you put on this dog?"

"On him? No price at all!" said the other. "I've worked ten days on him, beatin' him to a pulp every day, but I couldn't tame the beast. If you want him, you can have him for nothin'. Look out!"

Slaughter had crouched to spring, but the Carcajou merely snapped his fingers. "That's all right, brother," said he. "We're not going to have any trouble with one another. Steady, boy!"

Slaughter stood straight up and stared at this strange creature who spoke with the voice of a man but who had in its hands the iron grip of a bear's jaws.

And the dog stood quietly, waiting for the next move in the game, still murderous, still ready to battle to the death, but acknowledging the force of a mystery which could not be easily solved.

The Carcajou stepped to the heavy crate in which the

111

monster had been housed, broke out the iron bolt from the wood, and gathered the chain into his hand.

"We'll go downtown to get some new clothes, Slaughter," said he, and started off down the street.

Slaughter held back, planted his great feet against the snow, but the Carcajou walked on, taking slow, short steps, and the monster was dragged behind him.

"How long'll that go on before the dog jumps on his back and breaks his neck for him?" one of the men in the group of watchers said to the puzzled dog breaker.

"I dunno," said the dog breaker. "I talk about things that I know. I dunno nothing about gents like that one yonder. I never seen nothing like him before, and so I don't know." He still shook his head. "Look at the strength of him!" he pointed out. "That dog weighs two hundred pounds, and he's bracing every foot and leg of him to put on the brakes, but still Slaughter has to go along. I dunno. He held the neck of that brute like his hands were vises. I never seen nothing like it, and that's why I say I don't know!"

"Well, could the dog be made into something worth while in a dog team?" asked another man.

"You seen for yourself," said the dog breaker. "Slaughter is a dog team! He's sled dog and swing and leader all in one. But if you tried to make him part of a whole team, wouldn't he go and eat the other part?"

Only one man laughed. The others were too intently staring at the strange picture of the great dog as he gradually passed out of sight down the street through the white flurry of the snow.

CHAPTER 5
The Girl

THE LAW MIGHT BE SLIGHTLY BENUMBED IN DYEA, BUT it was not altogether dead, and therefore the Carcajou could not afford to linger in the town. Bill Roads would be out organizing a posse before long, for one thing. It was very strange that news, and Bill Roads with it, could move so fast. When he thought of this, the Carcajou felt a thrusting up of admiration in his heart for Bill Roads.

That man was a man, and no mistake about it!

There were some quick preparations to be made. He bought a new outfit of furs. Already he had acquired a sled, and the pack to go on it, with four excellent dogs. He needed merely to hitch up the dogs, put a thoroughly strong muzzle on his newly acquired monster, harness him in as sled dog, and strike out on the trail. He carried with him on this trip a burden of excess weight which few adventurers took with them. This consisted of an excellent Winchester rifle on the one hand, and under his coat a .45-caliber Colt revolver with the trigger filed off and the sights removed, also.

He would rather have traveled without one leg than without that revolver.

He went up Dyea Creek on the run. There was no need of urging his dogs along. He had a good leader that knew its business in picking out the trail, and the three animals behind the leader were constantly trying to hump their way through their harness, because behind them pressed the gaunt giant, Slaughter, red-eyed, silent, but slavering with hatred and rage and pure physical hunger.

It wanted, in fact, to get at those other beasts and destroy them. Very small, frightened, and frantic looked the four big Huskies as they tugged at their traces ahead of the dark beast. He looked to the Carcajou more than ever like a vast, long-legged rat. He was the ugliest creature that the man had ever seen. There was something more than animal ugliness—there was a spiritual hideousness about the brute that appalled the mind.

But the master was fairly pleased. He was more than ever pleased when it came to the terrible toil up the Chilkoot, where men labored inch by inch forward, groaning under their packs.

He put packs on each of the four dogs, another pack on his own shoulders, and what seemed to him a killing burden on the back of Slaughter. But Slaughter bore it lightly up the way!

He had before him the currying tails and quarters of the other animals, and his greed to get at them whipped him forward. He chased the dogs and carried his own mighty load. He also dragged with him the Carcajou himself, dangling at the end of a long chain.

Banner laughed a little, going up this famous slope at such a pace. In two trips he brought up the sled's load, and the sled itself. A man stopped him on the second trip.

"Is that a mad dog that you got there?" he asked.

"No, that's not a mad dog. He's only hungry," said the Carcajou. "Like him?"

"He looks like a ghost or a dog's nightmare of everything that no dog, or wolf, either, would ever want to be. Tell me truthfully, is he any good?"

"He's as strong as any two others. You can see for yourself."

"Lemme tell you this, chechahco," said the stranger. "You're a fool to take that big bundle of trouble into Alaska. There's enough trouble already inside; you don't have to take fire from the outside and bring it in! You'll burn before you been there very long!"

It was rather strange advice, but it was the only word of counsel that Banner received all the way. Other men regarded him not at all, except as an obstacle before them to be cursed or a trail breaker to be accepted with a grunt of satisfaction. But all that mattered essentially to John Banner was that he was working his way inside.

When he got to Sheep Camp he rested, as most other people were doing. It had been a strenuous time even for the limitless strength and the tireless nerve of the Carcajou. For he was learning a great deal that he never had known before. He was working at the fine art of snowshoeing. He already knew how to handle the ski very well from a certain strange and arduous winter of his youth, but he learned more and more about the same craft now. He learned the knack of tree felling and how to build camp in the most expeditious and comfortable way. He learned that a carefully made camp and a good sleep were necessary even to him in this country.

The rigors of weather and the trail wiped out the large margin which he could usually allow. In a more southern climate he could disregard such trifles as temperature. But in the white North it was a different matter. He could do more than other men, but he had to be careful. A bullet will kill the loftiest giant; and the North will kill the mightiest man almost as quickly as it topples over the weakling, unless brains and forethought are used.

115

But the Carcajou had this advantage: that he learned not only as a thinking, reasoning creature, but also in an animal sense. When an old-timer pointed out the signs of coming storm in the horizon mist, the Carcajou looked and listened and felt the lesson sink down into his innermost instinct. It was the same with signs on the trail. It was the same also with the handling of the dogs. By the look in their wind-reddened eyes he learned to guess what was in their minds; that is, in all except Slaughter.

That ugly monster was still a sled dog, pulling half the load, tireless as his new master, and hateful as a legion of demons. Every night came feeding time. Every night the muzzle had to be taken from the long head of the brute. And every time the muzzle was off there was likely to be a fight between Slaughter and the Carcajou. The man always won. He learned a wonderful adroitness in handling the spearlike thrust of those fangs; and yet he carried a dozen deep cuts even when he reached Sheep Camp. However, this constant battle pleased him.

Another thing pleased him when he arrived at the camp. This was to find that his reputation had preceded him. Reputation was the one thing he could not do without. Since he was fifteen it had always been with him. Since the day of his first battle, admiration, dread, and an invincible loathing always had surrounded him. Just as the great timber wolves slink from the path of the wolverene, so men shrank from the way of John Banner. And now they were shrinking again, even these fearless adventurers in the Northland.

He had traveled fast from Dyea. But rumor had gone before him on invisible wings. What he had done in Steuermann's was known, and how he had mastered Slaughter with his bare hands was known, also, although both of these tales had been immensely embroidered and built upon. Any tale worth telling by an arctic camp fire is worth telling well. As for those who doubted, one glimpse of the dreadful figure of Slaughter convinced that Northern world. They saw the hero carrying with him down the trail the proofs of his heroism.

Thus in Sheep Camp the Carcajou found that his fame was established even more firmly than it had been in the slums of New York, and the underworld of half a dozen cities. There was the same admiration, dread, and loathing. And he devoured this universal tribute with a savage and silent joy.

He could not be loved, he knew. Therefore he reveled in winning enormous hate!

Even the nickname had gone everywhere before him. That was best of all. Nobody knew him as John Banner. Therefore the law would not follow him so easily. It was always the Carcajou, now. Men who did not know the meaning of the word—and most of the men on the trail did not—nevertheless used it. It came to have a special meaning in their minds, more loathsome, more hated and feared than the animal to which it rightfully belonged.

At Sheep Camp Banner found the strange trio: the blind old man, together with Horn and Jimmy Slade. They had come in just before him, and he saw them unhitching a magnificent team of twelve dogs with two fine sleds behind the lot. It gave Banner a deep thrill of pleasure and suspicion to see the outfit. The whole atmosphere of it reeked with a suggestion of crime not very deeply hidden. There was some purpose in the minds of Slade and Horn that was not present in the mind of the blind man. What could that purpose be?

Well, whatever it was, it did not trouble the Carcajou. All weakness he despised. There was no mercy in him. The world gave him hatred; he repaid the world with contempt. Still, it was interesting to observe the trio and ponder on the probabilities of the future! A calm, deep voice spoke within him and told him that Old Tom had not very long to live at the hands of this precious pair.

The arrival of Old Tom was a considerable sensation in Sheep Camp, but not more so than that created by another outfit of a dozen dogs and three people that came in still later.

The dogs were as handpicked as those of Slade and Horn. The drivers were "Rush" Taylor, a wiry half-breed, "Bud" Garret, a famous dog-puncher in the North, and Anne Kendal, a twenty-year-old girl.

The Carcajou went over and looked at the outfit, standing close and staring at it. Slaughter, leashed on a chain and unmuzzled, stood behind him. They had just had their daily battle, and Slaughter, well-beaten, could be trusted for a time. It was pleasant to the Carcajou to parade the big beast without a muzzle; it was pleasant to turn his back on the monster while the men held their breath. No doubt they hoped against hope to see the beast attack the man with murderous power. What they hoped mattered nothing to John Banner, so long as he had their respect and their attention.

So he stood close while the other observers gave plenty of room to him and the four-legged thunderbolt chained to him. He looked with his calm, cold stare at the two men. It was a habit of Banner to let his eyes rest for a long period directly on the face of any one he chose to observe. Then, if they chose to resent his scrutiny, they could do so at their peril. That was all the better. In places where he was not known he had worked up many a pleasant fight by no greater maneuver than this.

So now he stared, according to his old custom, at the men. They made a formidable pair. They were as brown as wind and sun could tan their leathery hides. The white man was almost as dark as the half-breed. They were both big. They moved alertly and quickly even at the end of a long day's march.

It was clear that they were well-known. Other men in Sheep Camp hailed them by name, asked their destination, and when no answer came, began admiring the string of dogs.

But no one looked at the girl or spoke to her, and this was a great surprise to Carcajou. Certain ways of men in the North were still very new to him. But he knew little or nothing about women, north or south. They had not appeared in his life. They were unnecessary adjuncts. Now he looked the girl over with the same steady, grim eye he had used on the men.

She was almost as brown as her traveling companions; not beautiful, but handsome enough to give the illusion of beauty in this wilderness. It seemed that she was as much at home on the trail as either of her traveling mates. While they handled the camp apparatus, she went out and worked with the dogs, moving swiftly and fearlessly among the big Huskies. She had a certain touch and way with them that interested Banner.

Presently, standing with her hands on her hips, as though about to decide what she would do next, she encountered the eye of Banner, looked away, crossed her glance on his again, and suddenly let her eyes rest upon him.

That was very odd. Men had looked him straight in the eye from time to time in his life. Generally they had received enough attention later on to wish that they never had let an eye fall upon him. But never had any one considered him with the same perfectly cold detachment that she showed.

Charley Horn came up to Rush Taylor, the half-breed, and said quietly, but with iron in his voice: "You're following my outfit, Taylor. What d'you mean by it?"

"I go where I please in this part of the world, Horn," said Rush Taylor steadily.

"Maybe you'll please yourself too much one of these days," answered Charley Horn threateningly.

Bud Garret stopped his work and stood straight and still, listening.

"I mean you, too, Garret," said Horn. "We ain't gonna stand being shadowed the way that you've started out to do!"

Garret merely shrugged his shoulders. But it was plain that he was ready for action of any sort.

For a moment Horn's glance swung from one of them to the other, vengeance in his eye. Then he shrugged his shoulders and walked away.

The girl came straight to Banner.

"D'you think you know me, stranger?" she asked. "If you don't, my name's Anne Kendal. What's yours?"

He was both affronted and amazed.

"I don't carry excess luggage in the way of names," said he. "Any old name will do for me."

"You were staring at me as though I wore stripes," said the girl. "What do you mean by that?"

"People that wear faces will have them looked at," said Banner, and sneered at her.

Her eyes pinched a little with scorn and dislike.

"I'll take care of this bird," said Bud Garret, approaching hastily with a dangerous look.

Banner took a quick breath of relief. Any man was welcome as an opposite in the place of this girl.

"Back up, Bud," said she. "I don't want trouble started on my account."

"He's been staring at all of us," said Garret. "I'll teach some manners to the half-wit!"

"Look out, Bud!" called someone sharply. "That's the Carcajou!"

Bud Garret halted and suddenly grew pale. Then he stiffened his shoulders.

"All right," he said. "It ain't the first murdering carrion eater that I've handled in my time. I'll take him on!"

The Carcajou did not answer threat with threat. Nothing

abóut him moved except his lips. He wore a contented smile. He picked the place where he would strike home. That was all. But the girl stepped between them.

"This is my trouble," she said, "and I'll finish it."

She faced the Carcajou.

"What have you got to say to me?" she asked.

The Carcajou paused. There was nothing he wanted to say. There was only an emptiness in his mind. He could only sneer and keep it coldly sustained. But it was hard to meet her eyes. It was very hard indeed!

Suddenly he remembered what he had seen Charley Horn do, and shrugging his shoulders, he turned away and moved slowly off.

He went back to his own tent and began his cookery. He had hardly started when a footfall paused near him. Looking up, he saw a little gray-whiskered man well on in later middle age, who stared grimly down at him.

"Carcajou," said the older man, "I dunno where you was raised or what you got behind you. But up here this far north every girl is a lady until she's proved otherwise. After that she's a lady all over again. Don't you forget it, son, or you'll find more trouble than even your hands can put away!"

CHAPTER 6
A Job

THE OTHER MOVED AWAY; THE CARCAJOU SAT BEWIL-
dered. He had been talked down to; he had been taught
with a raised forefinger as though he were a child.

Yet he did not feel like leaping up and starting trouble
about this matter, because it occurred to him that there
might be certain unwritten laws in this Northland about
which he knew nothing. That little old chap would not
have dared to speak as he had done unless he were aware
that a vast weight of public opinion reenforced him.

It was a mystery to the Carcajou, except that he was
vaguely aware that there had been something admirable in
the girl's behavior. She had courage, directness, everything that he expected to find only in brave, resourceful
men of action. Yet he hated her with an emotion of sulky
helplessness that he had not felt since his childhood.

There was a tremor along his nerves and an aching in
his heart. The world seemed a bitter place, and he wondered why he had come to this wild Northland to find
refuge. Why should he not have gone, instead, to the Ori-
ent, where men are men and the women don't matter?

He gritted his teeth. American women were spoiled, he decided. Idle, uneducated, silly, proud, vain, useless creatures!

Then he remembered how she had worked among those big, wolfish Huskies without fear, doing more than any man other than an expert dog-puncher could have managed.

No, all that he said to criticize American womanhood did not apply to her—only the pride, the self-confidence, the disdain of others!

He looked back into his own heart. What were the qualities which endeared him most to himself? Why, there were pride, self-confidence, and disdain for the rest of the world!

If he criticized her, he was criticizing himself! As he reached this point in his conclusions he cursed between his teeth. The ache inside him grew worse, and there was a chill of fear along with it. He never had felt this way so long as he could remember. It was something like homesickness, a baffling disease of the mind.

A shadow sat down beside him. It was Charley Horn.

"Hello," said the Carcajou, and then stared in his own blank, lionlike way.

He remembered suddenly, as the other spoke pleasantly enough in return, that there were duties of hospitality which he never would have thought of in the old days, but they were sacred according to the unwritten law of this Northern land. Now he felt, whether he wanted to or not, he would have to pay attention to those traditional rules of the land of snow.

"Have some tea?" he asked. "There's another—"

"No tea," said Charley Horn. "I dropped over here to talk business."

The Carcajou nodded. He was not surprised to hear that Horn wanted to talk business. In fact, all of his dealings were with men of Horn's type.

123

"Business of what kind?" he asked.

"Day labor."

"Not interested."

"No?"

"No, not interested."

"I mean fifty dollars a day."

"What?" repeated the Carcajou, lifting his brows. "Fifty a day?"

Horn grinned.

"I wouldn't be offering your kind of a man pin money, would I?" he demanded, proud of the sensation which his offer had made.

The Carcajou half closed his eyes.

He knew perfectly well that Horn was a rascal, and that Jimmy Slade was another. But rascals were the only kind of men he was really familiar with. Again, the pair were up to some sort of sensational deviltry, and deviltry of that sort was what the Carcajou liked. Usually he played a lone hand, but here in the North he was on ground so new that he would hardly know where to turn for employment.

Finally, it would be amusing to find that he had come this far into hiding at great expense, only to find that he had fallen upon his feet, and that other people intended to pay his expenses for him.

This last item decided him.

"What's the job?" he asked.

"You'd consider it?"

"Yeah. I'll consider it."

"We've got a hard lot of work ahead of us. We're going down to Linderman and build a boat and cross the lakes. Then we hit the trail again. We want to build our boat fast, and we want to hit the trail fast."

"I'm no carpenter," said the Carcajou.

"You can pull at your end of a saw, though," said the other. "I guess that you could do that as good as any three men boiled down and put into one skin."

"All right, go on," said the Carcajou.

"That's all. We've got a good dog team. But we've got the blind old bat along with us, Old Tom, as they call him. He's got to be handled like so much dead weight of meat."

"How far do you let me in?" asked the Carcajou.

The other hesitated, then lifted his eyes from the ground and stared straight at his companion.

"We don't let you in at all. You're just a day laborer to us."

"Ah-hah!" said the Carcajou.

He also considered. For he was offended by this suggestion, and yet, along with his offense, he felt the great temptation of attacking a mystery, stepping deeply into it.

"It's this way. We want help along the trail up to a certain point," said the other. "After that we wanta pay you off and say good-by. We pick the point when we pay you off. It may be thirty days. It may be twenty, it may be fifty. We don't know."

"Fifty a day, eh?"

"That's our rate of pay. We'll give you twenty days' pay in advance to keep you interested."

"Oh, that's all right," murmured the Carcajou. "I guess that I can trust you fellows not to cheat me when the time comes for paying off."

"Yeah, you can trust us for that."

"You want me, and you want my dogs, too?"

"We want your dogs, except Slaughter. You can shoot that brute, far as we're concerned."

"He stays with me," said the Carcajou.

"We can't take you on, then."

"All right, then, you can't take me on," said the Carcajou, relaxing.

He glanced toward the great beast with redoubled hatred. Slaughter was separating him from an interesting adventure; but still he felt that there was more adventure in Slaughter than in the trio.

"Look," explained the other angrily, "the dog's no good. It'll tear somebody's throat out one day. You see if it don't. Whatcha want with that kind of a dog in your team, man?"

"Why, I like him," answered the Carcajou.

"Blast it all, Carcajou, won't you come without him?"

"Not a step."

"We'll have to take him along, then, because we want you bad, and your sled and your team."

Said the Carcajou: "I'll tell you this: that dog will pull a whole sled's weight all by himself. I won't let him do any killing in the team, if that's what you mean."

"All right," said Horn with a sigh. "We've got to have you, even if you've got Old Scratch himself along for a playmate."

"All right," said the Carcajou. "When do you start?"

"In eight hours."

"I'll be ready. One thing more."

"Well?"

"Why are the others chasing you?"

Horn swore, but he added: "Questions are one thing that you forget to ask on this here trip."

The Carcajou laughed softly.

"All right," he said, "that goes with me, too. You let Slaughter go along and I keep my face shut!"

CHAPTER 7
A Mystery

ALL THAT THE CARCAJOU REMEMBERED OF THE START, later on, was a voice that struck with a strange loudness out of the dimness of Sheep Camp:

"Now that they're together, you take and try to pick out a meaner three than them, will you? And may Heaven help poor Old Tom."

It was never the habit of Banner to take notice of offenses until they were offered directly to his face. And though this was almost under his nose, he was perfectly willing to allow the affront to pass.

On that occasion Jimmy Slade said: "I got a mind to look up the gents that are talking like that!"

"Why do that?" said the Carcajou. "If we ever start in hunting for all the people that hate us, we'll have to kill most of the world, I guess."

Jimmy Slade looked at him with startled eyes, said nothing, and presently turned back to his work.

So they pulled out of Sheep Camp and started relaying the outfits to the summit.

When that was finished there was little trouble in getting

127

over the nine miles to Lake Linderman, through a canyon bleak and barren, but frozen hard and offering good going for the sleds. From there on was the fine sledding of the lakes until they got to Tagish, where they would buy their boat, or build it, if necessary.

All of the first part of this trip was occupied with good hard work. While it lasted, the Carcajou made his estimate of his two younger companions.

They were both powerful men; they carried the extra burden of guns, and they knew perfectly how to use them; they had been in the Northland before, and were experienced in handling dogs and sleds and building camps. Their tempers were fairly bright. They never dodged labor, and worked well together at every task. It was only now and then that the murderous evil of their natures broke out in a glance, a few caustic or bitterly sneering words, or some explosion of sudden temper. On the whole they controlled themselves well, like men who have a great task in hand and are willing to put up with all sorts of troubles, including the presence of one another, in order to accomplish the end in view.

But the evil which he saw in them did not offend the Carcajou. It merely made him feel more at home. It warmed his spirit. It was a touch of that familiar characteristic which he knew best in life and among other men.

Moreover, he liked the physical vigor which they showed on all occasions. There was only one thing that displeased him, and that was their attitude toward Old Tom. When he was in hearing they were likely to express their actual thoughts in winks, gestures, a sign language, while their spoken words remained polite and gentle. It was plain that they did not dare to let the old man guess what they really were.

As for Old Tom, he was too much of a problem really to interest the Carcajou. He did not matter, and therefore he was dismissed. It was clear that through him the pair hoped to attain to some great end, but what that end might be was a mystery to John Banner. As far as he could see, Old Tom was simply an excerpt from a fairy story. He was always gentle, never raised his voice, never spoke in haste, never complained of cold or wind, insisted on getting out and running behind the sled, holding onto a line, whenever the footing was at all possible, managing himself wonderfully well on his feet for a man of his age, totally blind! Indeed, in every imaginable way he was as little trouble about the camp as a blind man could well be.

But blind he was, and why should a blind man attempt to reach the frozen heart of Alaska? What could he possibly gain there? Gold? But he could not even see the wealth he might be dreaming of! A friend? But what friend would wish to have this helpless burden placed upon his shoulders in such a land? Some familiar place connected with his past life? But in the howling wilderness there was no familiarity worth finding!

No, Old Tom was a great problem for the Carcajou, but since the fellow was old, blind, and therefore unimportant, he did not give any time to the solution of the difficulty. He used to feel that the most interesting moment of all was when, in an interval of quiet, brooding beside the camp fire at night, he saw the face of Old Tom harden suddenly and swiftly into lines that looked to the Carcajou like an expression of the most savage cruelty. Age and pain and the cruel affliction of the loss of sight were enough to embitter the spirit of the veteran, but it was only now and again, at long intervals, that he saw a glimpse, as through a frosted window, of the tormented soul.

The only incident of real importance on the way to Tagish was when Slaughter tore off his muzzle one day and killed three of the other dogs in the team in the few seconds before the Carcajou got his hands on the beast. The employers of John Banner gave him black looks on this occasion, but they said nothing. There was another of the endless series of the battles between Banner and his dog, and the incident was closed.

When they got to Lake Tagish, Slaughter performed again, and this time with the most unexpected results.

At Tagish they offered fantastic prices in their eagerness to get a ready-made boat, for it was feared that the thaw might come at any time. The frosty snow had disappeared from the face of the country; the limbs of the evergreens were no longer piled with white; and the river between the lakes was beginning to break up, the ice making noises that were anything from a cannon shot to a lion's roar.

However, since the thaw was expected almost momently, no one was willing to sell a boat, completed or almost completed. Men who were that far into the interior of Alaska felt that golden fortune was just ahead of them. They were smelling and tasting the treasure, as it were! They felt that they would soon be at the heart of it!

So no one would sell, and the three had to set to work building. They had to build a scaffold, and on this they placed great green logs, from which ponderous planks were whipsawed, one man standing above and one man beneath. That is, this was the way that Horn and Slade labored, but the Carcajou managed a saw all by himself, a little more clumsily because of the play that came in the saw blade after a wrong stroke, but when he mastered this he cut by himself more planks than the other two put together. Men used to come and watch him, the ceaseless pedal motion of his body from the hips causing them to shake their heads with admiration and wonder. If the thaw came soon, it was clear that the two partners would never forget this giant in their employ.

Three days after them arrived the girl with Rush Taylor and Bud Garret. All three set to work boat building, but it was apparent that they would soon be distanced; all their work on the trail would be useless if they were trying to keep up with Horn and Slade, unless the thaw on the lakes delayed longer than was expected.

But still the thaw did not come!

It was the night of that day when they had commenced to build the boat out of their green planks that Slaughter broke loose again. He was chained to the trunk of a tree, but broke the chain, and the light clanking noise of the breaking link of the chain was enough to awaken his master. The Carcajou got up at once. There was enough twilight for him to see the gaunt, powerful form of Slaughter standing over the place where blind Old Tom was lying. He could see the glint of the fangs of the brute, bared by the lifting of the upper lip, but Slaughter was making no attempt to tear the throat of the veteran. One hand of the old man was raised, without real strain or effort, and laid on the head of the dog; and under the quiet touch of that hand Slaughter stood still!

It was an amazing sight!

Gun in hand, the Carcajou waited, but he heard the voice of Old Tom speaking gently, and his bewilderment grew intense when he saw the great dog lie down beside the man.

It staggered John Banner utterly. He blinked and shook his head, told himself that he was a fool and seeing a dream, but there was the fact before him.

He strode to the spot.

"What are you doing to Slaughter?" he demanded harshly.

The shaggy head turned like a snake's to regard the master with hatred.

"Just talkin' to him, son," said Old Tom. "Ever try talkin' reason to dogs or men?"

The Carcajou muttered a savage, nondescript answer, and seizing the brute by the neck, bore Slaughter off to the tree, where the broken chain was refastened.

Then he went back to his own bunk and sat down in it.

Old Tom was propped up in his bunk, smoking. The Carcajou had heard that blind men never smoke, but here was a proof to the contrary. More than once he had watched Old Tom working at his pipe with every sign of satisfaction, and here he was again, puffing calmly, serenely, no doubt, thinking over again the events of that evening and the way in which he had established his mastery over the huge mongrel.

The Carcajou slipped down into his sleeping bag with a gritting of his teeth. He looked up at the dim tops of the trees, all sharply pointing like spears that looked straight up to the sky. The sky itself was nearer, and the world beneath it more vast and confused and mysterious than the Southern world which the Carcajou knew, the world of cities.

He felt a sense of depression and helplessness, a childish sense of helplessness only to be equaled by what he had felt that day when he had faced Anne Kendal in Sheep Camp.

But there was a different aftereffect this time.

Before he had been amazed and downhearted. Now he was swearing sternly to himself that he would penetrate the mystery and learn what it was all about.

To him nothing was as strong as strength. He had lavished force in the training of Slaughter and made the dog more dangerous every day. How was it that a comparatively weak old man could subdue the brute with a quiet voice and the touch of his hand?

CHAPTER 8
The Thaw Comes

THE THAW HELD OFF, UNEXPECTEDLY, SO THAT THE VERY day it came, Taylor, Garret, and the girl launched their boat. It floated at the most a quarter of a mile from the boat of Horn and Slade, and the latter fell into a frightful tantrum, when he saw the craft. But Horn merely said: "You can't make your luck over. And those birds, they ain't come to the real pinch yet."

He was handling his rifle in a significant way when he said this, and it was not hard for the Carcajou to guess that they meant murder when that "pinch" came.

"Luck? They've got the luck of Frosty Smith!" said Slade in answer.

"Who's Frosty Smith?" said the Carcajou.

They both looked at him askance.

"You never heard of Frosty?" asked Horn.

"No."

"Listen, Painter," said Slade to Old Tom. "Here's a gent that never heard of Frosty Smith!"

"All the better for him," said Old Tom with his usual calm.

133

"Frosty Smith," said Horn finally to Banner, "is the king of the thugs in Alaska. Is that right, Painter?"

Old Tom nodded.

"Nobody knows how many men have died because of him," said the blind man. "Or how many millions he's stole that other folks dug out of the ground! They used to say down in Circle City that we all did the work and Frosty had all the profit."

That name was to stick in the mind of the Carcajou, and to good purpose, at another time in his life.

In the meantime they were hoisting their square sail, made of odds and ends, and making good time across the lakes. The third day they lost sight of the craft of Garret and Rush Taylor, but that did not mean very much. In the open water their clumsy craft could not expect to gain very much on even a dishpan.

So they reached, in due time, the end of the lakes and Miles Canyon.

Horn was for letting the unloaded boat down the rough water with a rope and packing the stuff around to them later on, but Slade was made of sterner stuff. He pointed out that this was the chance for them to gain on the others or never!

Horn consented. He would run the rapids; and the Carcajou shrugged his shoulders. It was a point of honor with him that he should accept any venture that any other man dared.

So they bound big sweeps fore and aft, extending them on outriggers, and cast off from the shore a hundred yards above the mouth of Miles Canyon.

Below lay the more open water, but the frightful rocks of the Squaw and the thunder of the White Horse Rapids were below all. They would soon be swept through to safety, or else they would split and be overwhelmed by the terrible current.

* * *

What the Carcajou remembered of that passage through the white water was nothing except the grand, calm face of Old Tom as he sat quietly, with the shaggy head of Slaughter on his knees. They never needed to chain the dog when Old Tom was with him. And Slaughter closed his eyes and shuddered from head to foot while the spray dashed over the craft and the waters howled like a thousand fiends in the hollow canyon. But the face of Old Tom was unmoved.

The Carcajou, because he had the strength of more than one man in his hands, handled the forward oar, trying to keep the prow centered. But now and again, glancing back as they shot through a less dangerous stretch, he could see Old Tom smiling faintly, contentedly, with his head thrown back, and on his face the expression of one who listens to the most delightful music.

A dozen times John Banner knew that they were sliding from the piled-up waters in the center of the current, to be dashed to bits against the walls of the canyon; and a dozen times the rickety craft responded to desperate labor on the sweeps and continued safely on her way. These were miracles which were happening, but the miracles continued.

They saw the end of Miles Canyon, they shot through the Squaw, they roared into the thunder of the White Horse, and so into the peace of the lower waters. They were safe!

As they unshipped the sweeps, the calm voice of Old Tom said: "Well done, lads! Well done! I've only been through twice before, but I've gotta say that going through with your eyes shut takes you a pile longer than going through with 'em open!"

And he laughed a little, still softly.

"We'll see a girl and two birds like Taylor and Garret run the rapids like that!" sneered Horn. "We can lay up to the bank and take things easy for a while, I got an idea."

They tied up to the bank and cooked and ate a meal. As they boarded the scow again and loosed her down the river, another boat shot from the spuming mouth of the White Horse; a faint cry reached them through the uproar of the waters, and looking back as they made sail, the Carcajou saw the craft of their trailers, with Rush Taylor laughing and waving at the bows!

Slade handled his rifle with a hungry look.

"Not here!" said Horn sharply. "We got too much light of day on us."

But it was plain that they both meant killing. That was nothing to the Carcajou. Death was a small thing in this world, as far as he was concerned. What mattered far more to him was such a thing as the expression on the face of the blind man, looking with unseeing eyes down the river. The white North had left his heart clean. That was certain.

For the thousandth time the Carcajou wondered at him. There was a mystery deeper than anything Old Tom could guide his two villainous companions to; there was a secret of the soul which he possessed that they never could learn. Not that the Carcajou himself greatly cared to change—he merely wondered what the heart of this man could be like.

In all the years of his life he had told himself that one man is not much better than another. As for those who pretended to honesty and humane qualities, it was because they felt that hypocrisy paid them in the long run. Of that he was sure. He never had seen one person who would not take all possible advantages once he had the upper hand. Only in Old Tom he felt an imponderable element that dashed his surety. On those about to die, it was said that a peculiar grace descended, and there was something as profound as that on the brow of the veteran.

Horn and Slade were in close consultation by this time. They had failed once more to shake off the bulldog tenacity of those who pursued. Now they must attempt another shift as soon as they were securely out of sight of the others. With the first dimness of twilight they would try to run the boat ashore, unload it, cache a portion of the load, and sink the scow in the shallows. Then they would pack in as much as they conveniently could and make for their ultimate destination.

So for two days they struggled down the swift, yellow currents of the great Yukon, making sail where they could, laboring with the sweeps night and day, straining every nerve to get ahead.

Not until the second day, however, did they manage to get well out of sight of the other craft. Then as that brief night, which could hardly be called night, but rather a prolonged dusk, began, they beached the scow, unloaded her at once, sunk her at the edge of the water, and hastily packed the goods inland. They dug a good deep trench and buried a quantity of provisions in it, covering it over with saplings crossed and recrossed, so that even a bear would have had a great deal of trouble in opening up that cache.

What was left they packed on the backs of the dogs. There were fourteen of them now, including Slaughter, and they carried a stout burden, every one. Horn and Slade each took a heavy load; the Carcajou, with equal ease, bore as much as both the others, and even Old Tom insisted on taking a burden of some forty pounds. With this he went along fairly easily. He was given a rope connected to the collar of Slaughter, and it was an amazing thing to see the dog lead the man. It might well be that Slaughter had in him an evil spirit, but Old Tom had managed to find the way to tame him.

At any rate, there was never a moment when the beast was not ready to murder either dog or man in the rest of the party, but Old Tom he treated with more tenderness than a mother wolf would show to the youngest of her litter! When they came to an upward slope he leaned forward and helped the veteran up. When they reached a deep

137

rut in the ground he paused until the staff of Old Tom touched him, and the man was warned to prepare for the obstacle in the way.

Where a tree or a stump was ahead he swung wide and steered Old Tom past the danger, and from morning to night Slaughter tended Tom Painter with unending devotion; not that he learned how all at once, but during the three days they marched inland, steadily following the course of the Yukon, but keeping it a mile or more to the right, he gradually picked up a hundred arts of conveying information to the blind and helpless old man.

Horn and Slade and the Carcajou had fallen behind on that third day, and were watching Old Tom striding freely before them, while they commented on the strangeness of that performance.

"Dogs are just like safes," said Charley Horn. "All you gotta know is the combination to the dumb fools."

Slade turned his head at that moment and suddenly exclaimed.

"By the black heart of a witch, look yonder!"

Over a swale of ground behind them, striding through a thin growth of small timber, they saw a man, erect, with the bulk of a pack on his shoulders. Behind him came dogs, carrying packs also, and last of all another man and what might have been a boy—only it was not a boy. With one accord all three of them knew that it was Anne Kendal with her two companions.

They had picked up the trail again!

"Carry on," said Slade through his teeth. "They've found the trail again, and now the fools are gonna learn what else they've found. Charley, they gotta be turned back, and the only way of turning 'em is to use guns. Carry on now, but tonight we'll turn back and give 'em a surprise."

"All right," said the Carcajou, "and I'll do the surprising. I've got a grudge against one of 'em. And the whole three I'd like to show how—"

CHAPTER 9
Strung Up

WHAT WOULD HE SHOW THEM? HE HARDLY KNEW, EX-
cept that he felt that he had been scorned by them all, and
the proper answer for scorn is blasting wrath and the ir-
resistible strength of a right hand!

There were mysteries about him here in this Northland—the journey of Slade and Horn with the blind man
they hated and pretended to feel an affection for, the bold-
ness of Bud Garret in daring to affront him, the haughty
bearing of the girl, the unknown goal toward which all of
these people were striving. These made problems through
which he could not look, but of one thing he was sure.
That night he would attend to the affairs of at least one of
those who traveled in pursuit!

His offer was readily accepted. Horn merely said:
"We'll want you along, all right, Carcajou. But we'll be
there, too."

"I'll go alone or not at all," said the Carcajou calmly.

"Leave him be, you fool," said Slade to his partner
with irritation. "What d'you want more than a chance to
sleep sound and let somebody else do your work for you?"

140

Horn argued no longer.

When the twilight of the Far North gathered, they had increased their pace enough, and marched long enough, to leave the enemy behind them. Then they made their camp, the Carcajou ate a hearty supper, rolled himself in his blankets, smoked a final cigarette, and went to sleep.

"You forgetting?" Horn had muttered to him.

But Slade, more understanding, had snapped impatiently: "Leave him be! You gonna try to teach the Carcajou better tricks than what he knows already?"

The Carcajou closed his eyes in sleep contentedly at this moment, and for three long hours he slumbered heavily. It was the time he had appointed for himself, and at the end of that time his eyes opened as though he had heard the ringing of an alarm bell. He did not need to yawn or shake himself into wakefulness. He was suddenly and completely alert, and quickly dressing, he stood up in the icy chill of the night air.

It bit through his coat; it sank toward the bone like a cutting tooth, but he opened his lungs and inhaled a few deep breaths, and the strength of the cold fell away from him. A thin mist from the river had rolled over the land, rising to the top of the brush, but letting the trees stand up in little ragged islands here and there, with pools of paleness filling the hollows. It was a good night for such work as he had on hand, if only he could find the camp of the enemy.

He looked about him first and spotted Old Tom sleeping peacefully, his feet toward the embers of the almost dead fire, and the great dog, Slaughter, curled into an immense circle beside him.

He stepped up to the pair and stood over them, while Slaughter raised his villainous head and favored him with a snarl. But it was a silent snarl, a mere voiceless convulsion of hatred, as though the savage brute did not wish to break in upon the slumber of the man he loved.

141

Something of warmth touched the heart of the Carcajou.

Acts of thoughtful kindness were in his estimation the most absurd folly, and yet he found himself building up the fire again so that it could warm not those two rascals, Horn and Slade, but the old man, whose face was so weary and so serene!

Then, as though ashamed of this act, as the flames began to catch in the wood and rise, crackling with dancing sparks, he strode hastily out from the camp and started on his journey.

He had for weapons his Colt revolver, a good heavy hunting knife, and his hands. That should be enough, in light like this, that made distant shooting impossible.

But could he find the camp of the others?

It was amazingly simple. Not three miles back down the trail he heard a sudden clamor of dogs that led him better than a light; and then came a rush of savage Huskies about him.

The biggest and strongest and bravest of the lot came first with enough of the wolf—or the watchdog—about it to take a running leap at his throat. More than one man has been killed by the rush of wolfish Huskies in a strange camp. But the Carcajou laughed a little softly in the deep hollow of his throat, and picked the great dog like a football out of the air.

He got in return a double slash that opened his one sleeve of his coat from shoulder to elbow, and the other sleeve was torn straight across, just above the wrist.

But that was the only damage done. He kneeled beside the struggling brute and throttled him quickly into submission, while the rest of the team dogs around him scattered back. Their howling and barking fell to a number of frightened, high-pitched yelps. They retreated into ghostly outlines in the distance.

Suddenly a voice not more than twenty feet from the Carcajou said:

"There's something out there!"

And the voice of Bud Garret answered: "Yeah. Likely a wolf prowling. Look at them coward dogs come sneakin' back. The mongrels, they don't like the looks of a full-sized timber wolf. I tell you what I've seen—I've seen two real wolves chase a whole pack of sled dogs. Go back to sleep. I'm keeping watch!"

"All right. You keep your eyes peeled, will you? Maybe I oughta be standing watch myself all this time."

"We argued that out. You've done your half of the shift. It'll be real daylight before long, and this mist'll clear. But I guess they won't try nothing on us to-night. Even three like them need time to get up their nerve for murder!"

"The Carcajou, he needs no time. He's always ready to kill," said the half-breed. The talking ended, and the Carcajou smiled to himself with a heart filled with delight. This, to him, was as great a tribute as he could expect. It showed that men feared him even in this wild Northland. And what more did he ask from the world than fear?

As for what Old Tom got from Slaughter; well, that was another matter, a mystery which no ordinary man could hope to penetrate.

So he waited there on his knees for a full hour. Another man would have turned numb, and every nerve would have failed in the extreme cold and in that cramped position, but the Carcajou had the patience of a beast of prey, which must have patience if it is to live in the wilderness.

He would let that camp settle down completely before he moved again. In the meantime the dog in his hands did not move. It was not dead, but it squatted on the ground with eyes closed and with ears pressed back against its neck in a frenzy of icy terror.

At last Banner stood up, released the dog, and moved on. He glanced behind him and saw that the Husky had not stirred, but lay where he had put it, as though shot through the brain. That sight pleased him, also. Even dumb beasts could feel that there was a deadly terror in him—in his touch a fatal and cold magic!

He himself got down on the ground now.

He saw before him two or three red eyes, the glow of a dying fire. Then there was the shadow of a man sitting near the coals of the fire, a black silhouette cutting through the night mist, and facing directly toward the hunter.

The Carcajou moved inch by inch to the left, inch by inch until he had come through the half of a circle. He lay, finally, actually between the sentinel and the fire behind him. Not a sound did he make, and not a warning yip came from the dog team. Perhaps they had scattered too far and heard nothing?

He could see the girl in her sleeping bag on one side of the fire. He could see the half-breed on the other side.

Then he rose behind Garret and gave him the blow which he himself had received in Steuermann's. He knew it perfectly. It was delivered with the edge of the palm, and it fell across the top of the neck and over the two big cords that run up to the skull.

The head of Garret jerked back. He slumped sideways from the stump that he was sitting on. In one arm the Carcajou received the falling rifle. In the other hand he received the body of the man, lifted him, and stepped slowly, soundlessly, into the mist.

The trees thickened and blackened before him. He paused as his burden began to stir and mutter. So the Carcajou put him face down on the ground, gagged him, and lashed his hands behind his back.

He had plenty of cord for the purpose. It had been in his mind from the first.

Then he selected two trees a proper distance apart. He freed one of the man's hands and tied it well up the trunk of one of the saplings. Toward the other he stretched the right arm of Garret, and then drew the cord very tight.

Before he had ended, Garret was strung in the air with his weight on his tensely drawn arms, and with his toes barely touching the ground.

At present this was nothing, but after a time the weight of his body would wear out the strength of the arm and shoulder muscles. Then the full strain would come upon the tendons, and these, in turn, would begin to stretch. The real agony started at that moment. It would not take long. An hour or so of this would leave a man perfectly capable of walking, but his arms would not be fit for real service for a month.

Then the Carcajou stepped close and said at the ear of Garret:

"I was a murdering carrion eater the other day to you, Garret, and now I've walked back here through the night to tell you that it's a bad business to call names. Don't call names, Garret. Kill your man if you have to, but don't call him names! You can stay here a while and think it over."

Then he turned and went off quietly through the night. The pleasure of his adventure filled him to the throat with joy. He wanted to burst into song.

CHAPTER 10
The Blind Leader

WHEN HE GOT BACK TO CAMP, THE NOISE OF DOGS AGAIN showing him the way, he slipped back into his bed, and there he was found by the others when they wakened in the morning. Horn said dubiously: "Well? What happened? Have a good sleep all night?"

"All except a funny dream," said the Carcajou.

"What kind?" asked Slade.

"A kind that would make you laugh," said the Carcajou. "I dreamed that I went back about three miles and found their camp, and Bud Garret was standing watch, or sitting watch, rather. And I dreamed that I got hold of him and snaked him away and said to myself that one helpless man would be a lot worse for the others to handle than a dead man. So I tied him between two trees with a gag between his teeth. I tied him so that his toes just touched the ground and the whole of his weight was pulling on his shoulders. By the time they find him, I've got an idea that he'll not be able to use his arms for a month or so—if he hasn't strangled to death trying to work against the gag and scream for help."

146

He chuckled as he said this.

The other two grinned sympathetically.

"Got any sign that you really went into that camp and did all this?" asked Horn, however.

The Carcajou looked narrowly, earnestly at Horn, without making a sound in reply. But here Slade averted trouble, perhaps, by snatching up a rifle. "This here gun wasn't in our camp yesterday!" he exclaimed. "Look here, Carcajou! Did you bring away Garret's gun, along with him? A man in one hand and his gun in the other?"

The Carcajou, however, seemed to have lost interest in the conversation, but at this point Old Tom broke in: "D'you mean to tell me, Carcajou, that you tied up a man where he'll be tortured like that for hours, maybe?"

The voice of the Carcajou was a mutter that sounded like a low growl.

"How else would I do up a gent like Garret?" he asked. "Want me to ask him politely to turn back from our trail? Or would you like to have me kill him straight off instead? I wouldn't have minded doing that, but one helpless man will tie up his partner, as well. That was my idea."

Old Tom stood up straight and struck the ground with his staff. His empty eyes were turned under a depth of darkened brows toward the Carcajou.

"According to my lights," said Old Tom, "nobody but a mean hound and a low hound would do a thing like that."

The Carcajou rose from his food with his face perfectly calm, except for the slight lifting of his upper lip. Opposite him, and in front of Old Tom, rose the monster, Slaughter, and stood with a frozen smile facing his real master. But suddenly it dawned upon the Carcajou that ownership in the eyes of the law is a very small thing compared with ownership of honest and sincere affection.

Slade cut in at this point: "The Carcajou is a rough man, Tom. You know that by this time. But he's all right.

147

We had to turn 'em back, didn't we? They were gonna trail us right to the—spot, weren't they?''

The face of Old Tom was still stormy with wrath; but, fighting fiercely with himself, he controlled his speech.

"We're far north; it's a hard country," was all he muttered. "And I'd rather lose all the gold in the world than put another man through torture before his time!"

"Looks to me—" began Slade angrily.

Horn exclaimed: "Jimmy, shut your mouth!"

He made a significant gesture toward Old Tom as he spoke. And Slade controlled himself in turn. But all three were now glaring at Old Tom with a savage concentration. The same emotions that the Carcajou felt, he could see clearly mirrored in the faces of his two employers. That did not altogether please him. They were a low cut, he knew, and it was far better to be like Old Tom than to be like either of the younger men.

It was a very sudden check, an odd shock to the Carcajou, and it kept him in brooding silence for hours. It was not the first time that he had received a shock to the soul from the words and the behavior of Old Tom. It was not the first time that something in the dignity of the man overcame him with awe first, and with shame and hate later. He merely said that day: "I've loaned you my dog these days, and you pay me back as a dog would. You can get on without Slaughter from now on!"

So with his own hands he took Slaughter on the lead.

It was not a very convenient arrangement. It simply meant that either Slade or Horn had to walk in front of Old Tom that day, with a cord tied from the belt and running back to the hand of the veteran. But neither Slade nor Horn seemed to feel it strange that the Carcajou had acted as he did; neither of them appeared to bear the slightest resentment, and Slade actually said to the Carcajou:

"I don't blame you. We hate the old fool as much as

you do, and after he's brought us to—Well, listen to me, Carcajou. Me and Charley have been talking things over. If you've turned back the girl and her friends, it's a load off our minds. I'll tell you what—we ain't chasing this far north after any rainbow, brother. We're lookin' for the pot of gold. I guess you figgered that out a long time ago. And we want you to get a slice of the profits. Suppose we split the thing five ways. You get one way, me and Horn get the other four, because we had the idea first. Does that sound to you?''

The Carcajou only answered: "I've got three wishes.''

"What are they?'' asked Slade.

"The first one is that Old Tom were just half his real age; the second is that he had his sight back; and the third is that he should be forty pounds more of muscle.''

Slade grinned brightly.

"I know,'' said he. "You'd like to go at his throat, then?''

He chuckled again. "It's all right, son,'' said he. "Maybe you'll be even with him a long time before you think. Brother, me and Charley have pretty near choked over the old hound and his church talk!''

They traveled on slowly that day, and yet there was never a sign of pursuit. Even when the air cleared of all mist, and they reached a comparatively high knoll from which they could survey a great sweep of country, there was no trace of the train of pack dogs and people that had followed them the day before. The joy of Slade and Horn was great indeed! But the Carcajou could feel no pleasure in the praises which they heaped on him.

Watching Old Tom as that pioneer stumbled and staggered on his way, guided infinitely less by his human leader than by the dog on preceding days, a cold wave of shame swept over the Carcajou. Shame had been a stranger to him before his journey to the Northland. Shame was a thing which one felt, according to his code, after one had

shown the white feather, or had been outwitted or tricked
or beaten by sheer force by other men. Shame was the
emotion of the weakling, insufficient for the task in hand.
And the Carcajou never had been insufficient for the task
in hand.

But now he felt himself hemmed in and baffled and
beaten in a strange way. He would have given more not to
have taken the giant dog from Old Tom than to have un-
done any other act of his life. There were, indeed, few
things that he would have wished to undo in his long ca-
reer of successful crime. But this was different. And as he
watched the dog, constantly straining to get to the man he
loved, it seemed to the Carcajou, for the first time in his
existence, that some all-seeing eyes must be fixed down
upon the scene in judgment. What that judgment would
be he could guess with much wretchedness.

They came to a creek, at midday, running down to the
Yukon between steep, high banks.

"This ought to be the place," said Slade. "We've come
about the right distance down the Yukon, Tom, according
to your way of reckoning."

Old Tom stood on the edge of the bank and turned his
empty eyes from side to side. With haunted faces, Horn
and Slade watched him. It was clear to the Carcajou that
much hung upon this moment. Since he had been made a
partner in their venture, he should have felt some excitement, also. Strangely enough, that was not the case. With
a sort of melancholy disgust, he eyed the straight shoulders and the fine head of the old man.

"How does it come into the Yukon? About south,
southwest?" asked Old Tom.

"Just that!" said Slade eagerly.

"Is there a low bank on the north side, covered all over
with brush and a few small trees?"

"No," groaned the other two in unison.

"A bank like that could be washed away any season if

150

a flood came down,'' said Old Tom. ''Any fringing of trees on top of the bank across there?''

''Yes. There's a scattering of trees.''

''I think that it's the place,'' said Old Tom. ''Is there a big double bend of the bank off here to my left?''

''Yes, two big bends.''

''It's the creek,'' said Old Tom. ''It's Thunder Creek! And we're only a half day's march from the mine—ah, you told me not to use that word. I'm sorry!''

''That's all right,'' said Slade. ''The Carcajou's in the partnership now.''

''The Carcajou?'' exclaimed Old Tom.

He said no more, but the expression of his face was enough to fill the heart of the Carcajou with a hot wave of wrath, and then an icy shock of this new shame went through him.

He was beaten and depressed, but now his attention was taken up entirely by what followed. Old Tom had turned about and was saying: ''I remember that the wind that day was just east of south, and when I was lost in that fog, coming down the bank of the Yukon, I had to feel my way along till I got here to the mouth of Thunder Creek. When I got here I felt that I could hit out the direction pretty well. I figgered that it would take me about four hours of steady marching. The fog was so thick, blowing down the wind, that I couldn't see two yards ahead of me.

''But I had to get back to the mine. I was nearly starved. You remember, it'd been two days since I'd eaten? And marching along all of that time! Well, I knew that that wind prevailed out of the south, or a point east of south. I got the feel of it on my face and my hand and marched for four hours. I crossed about half a dozen creeks, got through a tangle of trees, and at the end of the four hours I started to cut in circles.''

He paused and shook his head.

''Go on!'' urged Slade eagerly.

"Why," said Old Tom, "just as I was about to cut for sign in circles, that fog lifted a mite, and the willows around me had a kind of familiar look. And all at once I understood. I'd been lucky enough to walk plumb onto the old mine! But I've told you boys this before."

"I could hear it a million times more," said Slade. "Now, you think that you could walk blind to that same spot?"

"If somebody can give me south by east, a point or two, I'll try to make it. Mind you, the map ain't as clear in my mind now as it used to be. I guess I'm stepping a little shorter, too, since I've lost my eyes. Suppose we make it five hours of marching and then stop and look around? But if we don't come out close on the spot, you'll have to start searching that swamp from head to heels, and that's no joke, I reckon! If I can't bring you right on the place, maybe you'll never find it in a life of searching. But I've warned you before. There's a hundred of those creeks, and every one of 'em the same; and every one of 'em with the landmarks washin' out and fillin' in every year, y'understand? It's a regular labyrinth. You'll see, pretty soon! Head on then, and give me the direction, and I'll try to measure out the right distance once more. Oh, for some luck! The folks back home certainly need it!"

CHAPTER 11
The Back Trail

MONEY FOR ITS OWN SAKE WAS A SMALL THING TO THE Carcajou, and yet he could not help being stirred by the possibilities that might lay ahead. As they trekked across the rolling miles in the hours that followed, he found occasion to say to Slade: "If the split is in five parts, one for me and four for you and Horn, where does Old Tom come off?"

"Why should he come off anywhere?" snapped Slade with an oath. "Ain't he old enough to die?"

He sneered as he said it, his eyes flashing, and John Banner looked straight before him, seeing the future and amazed because he did not relish it. It seemed to him as though a mist lay over his spirit, through which he saw all things dimly. He felt that he could not criticize Horn and Slade without criticizing himself, and he had never learned to sit in judgment upon himself.

They came, now, to a district shrouded in dark trees, all small and rarely growing closely together, but with heavy brush between. As they climbed a knoll they could look forward upon the gleaming face of a swamp that was

153

cut by the waters of scores of twisting creeks. It was such a tangle, even a compass seemed of little use in guiding one across.

But Old Tom was going confidently on, feeling his way a little with his staff, when Slade looked back and exclaimed: "There! By all the demons below!"

Looking back, the other two saw four Huskies come through a thicket not half a mile behind them, and after the Huskies, a small stripling carrying a pack.

It was the girl, then?

The brain of the Carcajou spun into a dark mist. He had the explanation easily at hand. The disabling of Garret had been enough to make the half-breed see that this trail was no longer practicable. Even Garret and Taylor together might have a hard enough time in facing the dangers before them, but those dangers were impossible for a man to combat single-handed. So Taylor had turned back, taking his companion with him; but the girl, dauntlessly, had gone forward! For there she was, trudging steadily on toward trouble.

"Go back and turn her around and start her toward the Yukon!" said Horn and Slade to the Carcajou. "Throw her into Thunder Creek and let it carry her into the Yukon, for all that we care!"

"I'll handle her," said the Carcajou.

He turned and hurried back with long, swift strides. The affront that she had put upon him long before still rankled in his very flesh like a poisoned barb, and it seemed to him a pleasant thing to stand before her on this day as master.

The others disappeared behind him into the brush; he went rapidly on, down a small hollow, and over the next swale he stepped fairly out before her.

She stopped, closed her eyes, drew away from him, and then pulled herself together with a mighty effort. The four dogs crowded about her feet, snarling at the intruder, and the Carcajou laughed with a sound like an animal's snarl.

"What were you gonna get out of this?" he asked. "Walking straight ahead, what were you going to get out of this? Tell me that, Miss Kendal?"

He heard the catch of her breath. She was looking at him as at a nightmare.

"I kept on because I'd gone too far to turn back," said she. "That's why I kept on trailing you."

"You can turn around and follow your own trail back into the Yukon, then," said he.

She made no answer to this, but eyed him gravely.

He waved his hands. One of the dogs jumped far to the side and yelped.

"Start going!" commanded the Carcajou.

Still she did not move. He laughed brutally, saying: "I gotta force you, do I?"

Her eyes were as steady as they had been back there at Sheep Camp, when there were plenty of people around her to support her, and at this he chiefly wondered, seeing the dismal emptiness of the landscape about them, and hearing the growling of the currents in Thunder Creek, not far away. He walked up close and towered over her.

"Start moving!" he repeated.

Nothing that he had ever seen in his life amazed him like what he saw now—for she was actually smiling up at him, though rather faintly.

"You can't do it," said she.

"I can't do it?" echoed the Carcajou, still more astonished.

"You could torture Garret till he was half mad," said she, "but you can't touch me."

"Oh, I can't, eh?" muttered the Carcajou. "You tell me why, will you?"

"People are made that way," said the girl. "A man

155

who can take another man as you took big Bud Garret couldn't lay his hand on a woman.''

He stared at her. It never had occurred to him that Garret was particularly big. A six-footer, to be sure, and with plenty of shoulders about him, but that was all. Bigger men than Garret, by far, had been as fragile reeds in his hands long before this.

''You're trying to now, but you can't,'' said Anne Kendal confidently.

''Why, you talk like a fool!'' he broke out, and strove to rouse his anger at her assurance, but anger was a cold, dead thing in him.

''I may be a fool, but you're not the demon people make you out,'' said this strangest of women, nodding at him. ''I guessed it the first time I saw you and heard your name. You're more man than carcajou. I'd be a thousand times more afraid if Horn or Slade stood in your boots just now!''

''There's a short cut to the Yukon, and that's Thunder Creek that's muttering over there,'' said he.

''Meaning that you could carry me over there and throw me in?''

''Well?'' said he.

She put her hands side by side and turned them palm up and looked down at them.

''I suppose you could,'' said she. ''But you won't.''

''I've taken a job on my hands,'' said he. ''D'you think that I'll come short of it because of you? What started you on this crazy trail, anyway? Your partners have turned back. If they're beaten, you're beaten.''

''They're beaten, but I'm not beaten,'' she insisted.

''Talk some more,'' said the Carcajou. ''Because I'm interested. I like to hear you. Talk some more, and tell me how you can carry on without a man to help you.''

''Perhaps I'm not without a man,'' said the girl.

''No?''

156

He swept the horizon with his eye.

"Where's any man?" asked the Carcajou.

"In your own boots," she amazed him by answering.

"In my boots?" said the Carcajou with a snarl.

"That's what I mean," she replied.

"I'm listening," he said. "There's a joke behind all this, I suppose. What's your idea?"

"My idea is that murdering hounds like Slade and Horn couldn't buy as much of a man as you are."

"They couldn't?"

"No, nor a scoundrel and hypocrite like Old Tom."

He started.

"He's not a scoundrel, and he's not a hypocrite," said the Carcajou.

It was surprising to him that he felt sure of what he was saying as of nothing else in the world—the virtues of Old Tom, whom he detested so!

"He's both things," said the girl. "You're merely pretending that you don't know it."

"I'd like to hear your proof about Old Tom before you start on the back trail along with me," said he.

"What sort of proof do you want?" she asked. "When a man lets down his partner and breaks his word, isn't that enough?"

The Carcajou shook his head.

"Old Tom never did that, never could do that," said he.

"I know," said the girl.

"How do you know?"

"The partner he let down was the husband of my sister."

"Then he lied," said the Carcajou brutally.

"Dead men don't lie," answered the girl. "He was dying when I heard him say it for the last time!"

CHAPTER 12
An Indian Tale

IT IS TRUE THAT DEATH SEEMS TO BRUSH AWAY FALSE-hood. The Carcajou, sobered, listened and looked hard and deep into her eyes. Suddenly it seemed to him that in this world of lies it would be almost as hard to doubt her as to doubt Old Tom himself.

Yet a lie must have existed as between the two of them. His eyes turned small with suspicious doubt.

"Well, go on and tell your yarn," said he.

"Jimmy Dinsmore was my brother-in-law!" said the girl. "He came up into Alaska four years ago for the first time. Then he went away and came back two years ago. He'd made a good stake the first time. He wanted to make a bigger one, because there were a wife and two children to be supported. So he came back last year. When he came home he had a hundred pounds in gold dust. That's over thirty thousand dollars, you know. But he talked as though that were nothing, as though he had millions in his pocket to spend, if he cared to, and the story he told was this:

"He'd heard an Indian tale about following down the Yukon and up Thunder Creek, a little tributary of the big stream. He went on this particular trail, and there he struck a huge marsh. While he prospected in it here and there, he ran out of provisions, and he could get at no game. He was close to starving when he happened to run across the camp of an old sourdough who had heard that same Indian legend and had beaten him to the spot. The Indian yarn was true. Jimmy Dinsmore saw the sourdough wash three hundred dollars out of one pan!''

"Hold on," muttered the Carcajou. "Three hundred dollars out of one pan?"

"Yes. Just that! Oh, you could trust Jimmy if you'd known him. He was the soul of honor. He stayed with that prospector for a few days, and the old man took care of him. Jimmy was half dead, and he gave him food and treated him like a father. He was absolutely square with him. Then one day the sourdough tried a shot at some birds near the diggings, and the shotgun exploded.''

She raised her hand to her face, which had twisted with pain. "He wasn't killed," she said. "But both eyes were put out."

"Old Tom?" exclaimed the Carcajou, immensely interested.

"Old Tom," she said.

He shrugged his shoulders. "This doesn't prove that Old Tom was a hound," said he.

"Not yet. You'll hear," said the girl. "The next thing was to get him out of Alaska, or far enough south to find a good doctor. It was the worst season of the year, but they had plenty of good dogs, and enough provisions to make the try, so they pulled out. It was a terrible march going out, but Jimmy was an iron man. He had to handle himself, and he had to handle Old Tom as well. It was a frightful trip. They had two dogs left when they mushed the last mile down to the sea. They got a boat and went to Seattle. Jimmy took Old Tom to a doctor, and the doctor said that nothing could be done. It was a hopeless case.

There and then Old Tom swore that he would reward Jimmy for sticking by him on the long trek out. He said that he would give Jimmy a half interest in the mine and let him go back and clean out the placer. It was a rich find. There was no doubt of that. One man could wash out a fortune in a single summer! And Jimmy was for turning about and going back straight into Alaska, but about that time he got a telegram from my sister in Portland, Oregon, telling him that the little boy was terribly ill. So down he came with a rush. Old Tom was to make out the legal papers and send them after him, giving him his share of the mine. Then, on the way down, in a steam-heated train, he caught a cold that turned into pneumonia. He was a mighty sick man when he arrived. I know, because I met him at the train."

The Carcajou, focusing his eyes beneath a frown, continued to stare at her.

"Go on!" he commanded harshly.

"I got him home," said Anne Kendal. "The next day he was delirious. The day after, he seemed a lot better. He told us all about Old Tom, and we began to watch the mails for the letter that was to come from Jimmy's partner. But the letter didn't come. Two weeks later Jimmy was well enough to sit up. The next day he had a relapse, and died in less than a week. And there was never a sign of a letter from Old Tom.

"I knew then that Jimmy was being cheated. He had saved the life of that old sourdough, I knew; and I knew, also, that half of the mine was no more than his rights. So, finally, with everything going worse and worse at my sister's home, I sold out my birthright and went to Seattle to look up Old Tom. It wasn't easy to trace him. But finally I located him, trailed him, and found him walking up a gangplank on board a boat bound for Juneau.

"Well, I followed him. He had two men with him that looked like criminals. They were your friends, Horn and

Slade. If you call them your friends! I took the next boat for Juneau, found the three there getting an outfit for the inside, and I decided that I would do the same thing. I have enough money to stake on one last try. Everybody recommended Garret. Through him I got Taylor, the better man of the pair. They bought the dogs and the outfit, and we loaded onto the same boat that carried the others to Dyea.

"Since then we've hardly had them out of sight. If there had been only the two of them, I would have won, too. But they came across you. That was their good luck. They persuaded you to join them. Otherwise, right now I'd have Taylor and Garret beside me, and their guns would clear the road if the road needed clearing. That's the story. I've finished."

He cleared his throat and said: "Either you're a liar, or your brother-in-law lied to you, or else Old Tom is the greatest faker in the history of the world."

"What d'you believe?" asked the girl.

He closed his eyes and thought. It was hard to doubt her and her straight-glancing eyes. But it was still harder to doubt the man who had conquered Slaughter with a touch of his hand.

"Old Tom is not a faker," he said finally, shaking his head.

"Good for you!" murmured the girl.

He was surprised to see her eyes shining.

"You like him, and you stick up for him," she explained. "And there's nothing better than that. I knew you were the right stuff, even if they call you Carcajou. I know you'll do right by me."

"What would doing right by you mean?" he asked her.

"Let me stand in front of Old Tom and tell my story, and see if even a blind face can keep from admitting the truth!" she exclaimed.

The Carcajou started. It seemed, at first glance, a quick

161

and too simple a defeat for him. On the other hand, he was tempted by the thought of seeing the two of them face to face, the girl and Old Tom, both, apparently, so dauntlessly devoted to the truth. The thought made him smile.

He had always felt that honesty is only a mask which some people are able to wear more effectively than others. He was sure of it now, in looking forward to that encounter. Either the girl lied, or Old Tom was a consummate cheat! To be sure, he had half the value of an incalculably rich mine to influence him. But the girl had the same idea to influence her.

Should he believe the man or the woman? He hesitated and shrugged his shoulders. When he looked at her again he saw that she was smiling, and she explained:

"I wanted to see you blasted off the face of the earth when we found poor Bud Garret tied between the trees this morning. Then I started hating Bud when he begged Rush Taylor to turn back with him and not to go on when there was such a thing as the Carcajou ahead of them. But now it seems to me as though the whole thing were planned out for me by a good jinni, because I can see the Carcajou will give poor Molly better justice than both Garret and Taylor put together."

"And who's Molly?" snapped the Carcajou.

"Why, Molly's my sister," said the girl with an air of surprise.

The Carcajou frowned. It was all too simple and virtuous. "Nothing for you to gain yourself in making this long march?" he asked.

"Except to see Molly well fixed. No."

"Bah!" grunted the Carcajou in disgust.

She shrugged her shoulders, and then looked straight back into his face.

"You're smiling at me. You're mocking me right now," said he angrily.

"I'm smiling," said she, "because I know that you'll

help. Brave men are never wrong. They're always on the right side.''

He glanced back through the annals of his life—with its scent of gun smoke in the nostrils, and the sickening odor of red blood spilling all the way across a table.

Brave men were always on the right side? Well, he could have told her a few little incidents in which they had been upon the side of death and destruction for its own savage sake. But he merely said: ''You think I'll go with you on that trail and catch up with 'em?''

She nodded. He drew in a quick breath. He wanted to swear, but his tongue was tied.

''If I put you in front of Old Tom,'' he said, ''will you promise to tell the same story you've told me?''

''Promise? I'll swear!'' she exclaimed. ''Do you think I've made it up? Oh, if there were light in his eyes, I'd make him blench!''

He looked about him at the gloomily rolling landscape. Even where there were trees, there was little green along the boughs, as though life feared to show itself openly to so cold a world.

Then he shrugged his powerful shoulders again.

''Come on with me,'' he said. ''I may be a fool, but I want to see which of two honest people is the liar!''

CHAPTER 13
Gold Dust

It was not hard, of course, to trail Old Tom and the other two men. If there had been any difficulty, it was removed by a sudden outcry not far ahead, a wild and wailing sound which, nevertheless, was not one of lament, but rather of maddening joy.

"They've found the place," said the girl. "Though how a blind man could lead them—"

"I've heard of things like that," said the Carcajou. "And blind men able to find things in houses they haven't been in for half a lifetime, too," he added.

They hurried on. To the voices of the men was added the wild howling of dogs, and the pack of Huskies of Anne Kendal began to yelp as though they were on a wet blood trail.

Presently they broke out from the trees into pandemonium. It was only a small clearing extending from the edge of the creek over a low hummock, with the remains of a shelter hut on the top of it. Over that hill the dogs were racing or rolling to get off their packs, some of them leaping up and down or sitting to point their noses at the sky, some bristling their neck fur and howling with a melancholy abandon.

Their frenzy was nothing compared with that of Slade and Horn. Staggering drunkenly back and forth, they shrieked and howled. It was as inarticulate as the yelling of the dogs. They clapped one another on the back. They laughed till they cried. They flung up one hand and brandished clutching fingers as though they were trying to tear the blue out of the sky. But each kept one hand close to his breast, palm up, and from time to time they stared down at the contents of that hand.

The Carcajou, approaching the clearing, had stepped out a little ahead of the girl. When the pair saw him, they did not pause to ask how he had managed with the girl. They simply rushed at him, babbling madness and joy. They thrust out their hands, and he saw the gleam of yellow dust in the hollows of their hands.

Horn raised his own few grains of treasure and flung them far, drunkenly laughing.

"You dunno what it means, Carcajou!" he yelled. "It means the yarn was true. The stuff is here. Whoever in the world seen a lay like this? Gold that ain't behind a steel door with a combination lock, but gold that's salted away through the ground like so much grit. Look, man! Look, look!"

He dragged the Carcajou to the edge of the running water, tore up a bit of the peaty soil, put it in the hand of the other, and forced him to hold the clod in the running water. As the ground disintegrated, the yellow stain of it floating down the current, there remained in the hand of the Carcajou two or three pinches of bright, glittering gold dust.

He had handled plenty of money before; in large sums, too, but never had it had such an effect upon him. Money was a social product, along with jails and the other tools of the law. Money was a thing to be desired, but for which

one had to pay either with labor or with crime, or with
both. But this was different. Here was gold which the bare
hands could take from the earth; here was gold growing,
as it were, out of the soil. It was like coming to the head-
waters of the river of happiness and prosperity.

Then a savage aftermath of emotion overwhelmed the
Carcajou, and he looked up with sullenly savage eyes, like
a dog which has found food and is ready to defend it from
the rest of the pack.

They had offered him one fifth share in this, had they?
And he had accomplished the great feat that baffled the
others—turning back Garret and Rush Taylor? He would
see these partners of his in perdition if he did not get a
larger share!

Horn, ordinarily, only forced himself to a decent attitude toward Old Tom. Now, however, he lunged for the
old sourdough, shook him by the arm with a mighty grasp,
and into his hand pressed the particles of gold he was
holding.

"You don't need your dog-gone eyes now," shouted
Horn. "There's something you can buy new eyes with.
There's something that will buy you everything you want
in the world. Except youth, Painter. It won't buy you that!
You're that much closer to the infernal regions, but you
can brighten up the rest of the way downhill."

Old Tom lifted his face, and the dark hollows of his
eyes turned up like the glance of a statue, in vain.

There was trouble in him, not pleasure.

"When I hear you yammerin' like this, Charley," said
Old Tom, "I don't hardly recognize your voice. It's like a
wolf howlin'. It's like murder. I've heard men yell before
they started to shoot. And they sounded the way you sound
now. I remember it made me pretty giddy and sick, too,
when I found that stuff. I got more'n four hundred dollars
in one pan. I got more than a pound of gold in one pan!
Not average, mind you, of course, but in one pan I picked

up more than a pound. That's worth a day's work, lads, I guess?''

He laughed a little as he said this, but he was not overwhelmed by his emotions. Instead, he was as calm as could be, and at ease. He merely smiled at the frantic excitement of the other men, which had driven even the dogs into a frenzy.

And a thunderclap came in the brain of the Carcajou as he asked himself what Old Tom had that was worth so much that he could actually despise a vast fortune in raw gold? No, Painter did not despise the money. He had worked hard years before getting to it. But it was an end subordinate to other ends more important in the life of the sourdough.

What ends might those be?

The Carcajou shook his head and sighed a little. He let the gold dust spill out of his hand. He almost forgot the water behind him, the world about him, for the sake of staring at the illumined face of the blind man. For there was a secret, the Carcajou knew, worth far more than gold or diamonds.

A yell came from Horn: ''Look! There she is! Carcajou, I thought you was gonna either turn her back or throw her into Thunder Creek!''

She was coming slowly down the slope from the edge of the woods toward the edge of the rushing water.

''Carcajou, what's the meaning of this?'' roared Slade in turn. ''But I'll handle her!''

''Hold on, boys! Hold on!'' exclaimed Old Tom, fumbling vainly in the air before him, as though trying to find the cause of the trouble. ''What's wrong? If it's a girl, don't yell at her like that!''

''Back up from her, Jimmy,'' said the Carcajou to Slade.

He had only delayed long enough to watch her manner of encountering a man like Slade when the latter was simply a hysterical animal. Now he saw, and he was covered with admiration. She was not afraid, it seemed. She merely stood still and faced the rush of Slade.

"Come back here, Slade!" shouted the Carcajou.

Slade yelled over his shoulder: "I'll come back when I've taught her the way to start back for—"

He grabbed her by both arms. His head was wavering from side to side in the excess of beastly joy and triumph.

"You'd foller us, would you?" shouted Slade. "I'll teach you to foller. I'm gonna make you a blank, Annie, my dear, and if—"

The Carcajou took him by the nape of the neck and squeezed. It was not a pleasant trick. Nerves were crushed against strong tendons, and tendons against the neck bone. Once when he was a boy a grown man with a powerful grasp had done the same thing to the Carcajou, and he had practiced all his life to gain a grip so strong that it would cause white, shooting flames of agony to dart up through the brain and paralyzingly downward through the body when he tried the same maneuver.

Jimmy Slade gurgled in his throat and fell on his knees, with both hands raised to thrust away the remorseless pressure of that strong hand.

The Carcajou sneered down at him with a brutal complacence.

"Don't go grabbing people, Slade," said he. "Because this is how it feels sometimes."

He released Slade. Then he said to the girl: "Now you explain what you meant by calling Old Tom a traitor and a crook who didn't keep his word, will you?"

Savagely she faced the old sourdough, and Old Tom was now coming slowly toward them, fumbling with his staff and resting his left hand on the lofty, powerful shoulders of Slaughter, for the dog had been given back into his hand when he started up Thunder Creek to find the mine if possible. A very odd picture he made as he came with trouble expressed on his face.

And the girl said: "If you're Tom Painter, you've done everything I say. You've cheated a man who might have let you rot in the snows right here!"

"Cheated?" said Old Tom in distress. "Cheated, did you say, ma'am?"

His eager humility did something queer to the heart of the Carcajou. He pinched his lips together and stood there, searching their faces, looking from the face of the girl to Old Tom. One of them lied, of course. Both of them seemed perfectly brave and fearless in their integrity, but the very point of their debate proved one of them had lied and was still lying!

Which could it be?

Charley Horn rushed up, shouting loudly: "Don't talk to her, Tom. Don't say a word to her. Don't believe her. She's crazy. She's a crook!"

But Slade chimed in: "Aw, let them have their confab, anyway. What difference does it make to us?"

But he added: "Unless *he* turns crooked on us and tries to help 'em out!"

"He's not a fool," said Horn.

"Who are you?" Old Tom was asking the girl.

"I'm the sister of Jimmy Dinsmore's wife."

"By thunder!" cried Old Tom, and came toward her, stretching out his hand. "Are you really?"

"You detestable hypocrite, keep away from me!" she exclaimed, and he stopped, stunned by what he had heard.

CHAPTER 14
Cleared Up

"I<small>F</small> YOU'RE J<small>IMMY</small> D<small>INSMORE'S</small> SISTER-IN-LAW," SAID Old Tom, "you've got no right to speak mean to me, I guess."

"No?" she asked, savage with anger.

"If Jimmy were here—" said Old Tom.

"You know well that he can't be here!" said she. "You know well that he's dead and in his grave."

Old Tom caught his long staff with both hands and leaned upon it.

"Jimmy Dinsmore dead!" said he.

"Ah," cried the girl, "he loved you. He was never finished talking about you and the fortune you were going to make with him. And you left him to die, his wife and youngsters stripped of everything, except a little saved from what he brought home. Why did you do it?"

"Why did I do?" exclaimed Old Tom. "Are you Anne Kendal that he was always telling me about?"

"That's my name. Poor Jimmy!"

"I wrote to Jimmy; I wired to Jimmy. Why didn't he

ever send me an answer? Did he die then right after he got back, my poor partner?''

"What address did he give you?" asked the girl, her voice sharpened by hostility.

"He gave me No. 714 North Shore Drive."

"That's the right address," said Anne Kendal.

"But wasn't he there to get the letters or nothing?"

"I was there when he was away," said Anne Kendal. "Either my sister or myself. Never a word came from you. Why do you pretend? Why don't you admit that your greed made you go back on him?"

He sighed, murmuring: "Poor Jimmy Dinsmore—dead! Poor old Jimmy!" Then he added: "How am I cheating Jimmy?"

"By throwing him off and running away to locate the mine with other men!" she challenged.

Still the Carcajou looked eagerly back and forth from one of them to the other. Before long now the truth would come out in its ugly nakedness, and one of them would go down—Old Tom, no doubt, unless all the fire of this girl was the merest pretense.

A savage excitement possessed the Carcajou; it was better to him than watching a fight to the death between two fierce men. Whatever the result, it would prove to him that one of them was a scoundrel. Of the two only honest people in the world, only one would remain! The rest, all the rest, were wretches like himself; criminal wretches, too, if they simply had the strength to turn desire and conviction into acts!

They were all like the Carcajou—all the rest! That was the grimness of his satisfaction as he watched this debate. From one face or the other, the mask was now about to be stripped.

Old Tom had paused to consider her last remark. The length of the pause convinced the Carcajou that the blind man was the villain. Men do not have to pause so long, he said to himself, when they have free consciences and open hearts.

"Jimmy Dinsmore," said the sourdough, "was the last man I ever knew with my eyes as well as my ears. I depended on eyes, Anne Kendal, after all those years of prospecting. Slade and Horn had stuck by me through thick and thin, but you tell me why I would throw over Jimmy Dinsmore and give a half share to these two, will you, if I could have got in touch with him?"

"Nothing but diabolical spite!" said the angry girl.

"Were you in town all last year?" he asked her suddenly.

"Yes, all the time."

"If you didn't get any letters, any telegrams—and that I don't understand—how come, then, that my advertising in every morning and evening newspaper didn't get to your eye? Big, black-letter print, asking for information about Jimmy Dinsmore, describing him, and offering a reward?"

"How can you say such things?" said the girl, more and more indignant. "A thousand people knew Jimmy. One advertisement would have been enough!"

"Charley," said the old man, shaking his bewildered head, "you know how many letters I dictated to you, how many telegrams you wrote out for me, and wasn't the bill for the advertising more'n fifteen hundred dollars?"

Charley Horn scowled at the face of the blind man, his upper lip curling. He answered nothing at all.

"You can give 'em your word I've told the truth, Charley, eh, boy?" said Old Tom.

The Carcajou, catching at last at a new idea, whirled sharply around and glared at Horn.

Then Jimmy Slade cut in: "Why, you old fool, you were sold from the start. You were sold out from the beginning. D'you think that we weren't playing you for a long chance? Why else would we've trailed up here with

172

you? You simply led us to the right spot, but dog-gone little good you'll ever get out of it, you half-wit.''

Old Tom freshened his grip on the staff on which he was leaning.

The great dog, Slaughter, looked suddenly up and licked those weather-browned hands.

Understanding rushed on the Carcajou, on the girl, on Old Tom, in a single instant. Then Anne Kendal said:

"I see what happened, Old Tom. When Jimmy Dinsmore lay there dying, groaning, cursing his luck because he had to leave his wife and the youngsters behind him unprovided for—all that while, all those terrible days, he might have been at ease. Is that it? But this—this Charley Horn was lying to you all the while?''

"Charley, the chills that I've had up my spine about you now and then, they were the truth, weren't they?'' asked Old Tom.

"You've talked enough,'' said Charley Horn.

He turned to the Carcajou.

"Now, Carcajou,'' he said, "you and Slade and me had better step aside and talk this here thing over. We've got a pair of 'em on our hands. There might have been only one, if you'd done your job and turned the girl back. It was a fool thing to let her come through. Now there's two of them that've got to be handled. We'll have a sit and talk it over.''

"We don't need to talk,'' said the Carcajou.

"You got a bright idea already?'' asked Slade eagerly.

And he ran his eyes curiously over their hired man, as though finding and admiring infinite possibilities.

The Carcajou took from his pouch a thin, sausage-shaped canvas bag, filled with the gold dust which was his advance pay, and threw it at the feet of Slade.

"I've made up my mind,'' said he. "There's your share in me. You can have it back. I stand with the girl and Old Tom. I've done my share of hard things and crooked

173

things, old son, but it seems to me that I'm stopping short of the pair of you."

Horn gasped: "Hey, Carcajou, you're crazy. You dunno what a placer like this means. Millions, likely; millions, man. D'you hear me?"

"Why, sure," said the Carcajou. "I hear you well enough. I've heard dogs bark before; I've heard them growl, too."

He made a gesture, while they gaped at him in astonishment.

His gesture indicated the girl, who was standing petrified with amazement at the side of Old Tom, her two hands affectionately clasped about his arm.

"They're honest, Slade. It's the first straight up-and-up pair that I ever drew at one deal in my whole life, and I'm going to play out this hand with them."

"It ain't really possible!" said Slade.

"He thinks he can slide us out of the picture, the fool," shouted Horn. "He thinks that, and then he'll try to pass them out of the picture after us, and have the whole caboodle for himself. But the fool don't think that we—"

He went for his gun as he spoke. It was not clear of leather before his hand stopped, and he stared bitterly at the blue-black length of the Colt that glistened from the fingers of the Carcajou. The latter held the gun carelessly, a little above the height of his hip, and thrusting forward half the length of his arm. His thumb had raised the hammer of the weapon and held it with familiar ease. He made no effort to glance down the sights. By touch and the instinct of long practice he would do his shooting, if shooting there had to be.

Both Slade and Horn stood frozen before him. "Old Tom, I've got 'em on the draw," said Carcajou. "I've got 'em stopped. Now you tell me what to do with 'em, will you?"

And Old Tom broke in: "Carcajou, I've been thinkin'

that you was a pretty mean, rough customer. But I dunno but I'm the greatest fool in the world when it comes to readin' character ever since I gone and lost my eyesight. What to do with Charley and Jim Slade? Dog-gone it, Carcajou, I don't know. If they're what they seem to be, if we turn 'em loose, they'll try to knife us from the bush. If we don't turn 'em loose, we've got to watch and guard 'em here, and that would be a pretty hard job, Carcajou. I dunno what to say.''

"Disarm them," said the girl, "and then let 'em go. If they try to come back, we have enough dogs about to spot 'em.''

"Take their guns, then," said the Carcajou briefly to the girl. "Take their guns and let 'em go. I might have known that that would be your way with the pair of 'em. But they were aiming straight at murder, and I'd give them what they wanted to give Old Tom—a bullet through the brain. But go get their guns while I cover 'em. You fan them, will you?''

He added sharply: "Turn around, the pair of you, and keep your hands up. Keep trying to touch the sky, will you?''

One revolver apiece was all that she took from them.

"Keep your hands up, and now start for that brush!" said the Carcajou. "Faster, faster!''

He began to shoot rapidly. The bullets struck the ground at their heels, driving stinging volleys of grit against their legs. Suddenly, capering, bounding, they rushed with a loud yelling into the shadowy bushes and disappeared.

CHAPTER 15
The Comeback

SEVEN DAYS FOLLOWED BEFORE THE END, AND THEY meant, to the Carcajou, seven steps toward a strange heaven. He learned a number of things with mysterious speed.

In the first place, in a single moment, by one act, he had destroyed the suspicion and disgust with which Old Tom and the girl looked upon him. In the second place, once they accepted him they opened their hearts and minds to him. And that was the way to the new heaven for the Carcajou.

He had not known before what it was to talk freely with another human being. There were always doubt and hesitation. Contact with other people had been always war, a war of wits, craft, or savage strength. He had won many a battle, and now he hardly knew how to adapt himself to the society of people who accepted his naked word as though it were gospel. He responded as one entranced.

They worked hard and through long hours. The plan was to gather what they could in a month, and then take up the out trail. Now that they had the bearings of the mine accurately taken, they could send in a crowd of hired laborers. So the Carcajou was always toiling. The girl did the cooking; in between meals she came down and helped in the washing of the dirt; they began to take out three, four, five thousand dollars a day. Wealth of incredible proportions began to loom before their eyes.

They had to labor, moreover, with all of their attention alert. It was true that Slade and Horn had been driven off, but they were not very far from the Yukon, and boats were many on the great river at this season; it would be strange if they could not get new weapons and perhaps return with reinforcements.

That was still in the minds of all three of them when they sat down outside the shelter hut for the second meal of that seventh day. They finished eating, and sat about drinking cups of steaming, strong coffee. Slaughter, lying across the feet of the blind man, was sleeping, and suddenly the Carcajou leaned and laid his hand on the dog's head.

Slaughter wakened like the wild thing that he was. A twist of that snaky head and he had the forearm of Carcajou in his jaws; one crunch of his teeth would ruin that arm forever. The girl sat frozen. Old Tom, unaware of anything, was continuing calmly in a yarn of the early days. And so the Carcajou waited, looking steadily into the eyes of the dog.

Little by little the green gleaming disappeared from the eyes of Slaughter. At last he relaxed his grip. Head high, ready for a spring, he silently showed his long white fangs to the man. But the Carcajou reached out again and laid his hand once more on the ugly head. The head sank down; the Carcajou patted it gently, drew back his hand, and for a long moment he and Slaughter stared at one another.

The story of Old Tom halted suddenly. "Ah, something's happening," he said. "I kind of feel it in the air."

"John and Slaughter have made up," said the girl. "He let Slaughter take his arm in his teeth. Why, John, that's pretty brave! Look there! Slaughter's wagging his tail a bit."

"You trust a dog or a man—it seems to do something to 'em," muttered the Carcajou. He stood up.

"I've got to be getting back to work," said he.

"Wait a minute," answered Old Tom. "I've been talking things over with Anne, here. We both think, and we both know that you ought to have a share in this mine. A fair share. Does a third sound right to you, Carcajou?"

"I don't like that name," said the girl.

"Nor me, neither," said Old Tom. "Does a third of the thing seem right to you, John?"

John Banner shrugged his thick shoulders. There was a puzzled look in his face.

"I was working for Horn and Slade for fifty dollars a day," he said. "That's plenty for me. I didn't come inside to try to find gold. I came to keep low for a while. That was all. I'll take wages, not a share in the gold we wash."

Old Tom cried out in husky protest.

"You're washing forty days' wages every day!" said he. "We can't cheat you, son!"

"We'd have nothing, nothing at all," said the girl. "Except for John Banner, we'd both be dead, I suppose!"

"You'll take a third. You oughta have a half," said Old Tom.

Dimly, like the voice of a stranger speaking far off, the Carcajou heard himself saying: "I stick by what I've said. I don't want a dead man's share of this, or yours, Tom, or yours, Anne. I'm a day laborer, that's all."

He had turned from the shack down the slope toward the creek when a scattering sound and a clamor of dogs broke out in the brush. As he stopped, staring, Anne Kendal said: "They're after a rabbit again."

"No, they're scared of something," interpreted Old
om.

Then there rang out from the bushes the unforgetable
oice of Bill Roads, that patient hound of the law, yelling
xultantly: "Shove up your hands, Carcajou, because I've
ot you covered over the heart! Shove 'em up!"

What the Carcajou might have done would have been
ard to tell, for on the heel of the call of Bill Roads a rifle
ang in the ambush, and the Carcajou felt a hammer blow
n his left leg. It turned numb, and he slumped heavily to
he ground. He had drawn his revolver in falling, but it
pilled from his hand as he tried to break the shock of the
all with his arms. It rolled half a dozen feet away down
he slope.

"Don't do that!" shouted the voice of Roads. "You
ound, that's murder. That ain't the law."

The voice of Charley answered: "You take chances with
im and you're a fool. I wish I'd got him through the
eart, but I got buck fever and shot too low, I guess!"

They came hurrying from behind the trees; Roads first,
vith Horn and Slade behind him, rifles in their hands. Old
om, feeling before him, found the fallen man and gripped
im.

"Are you hurt bad, son?" he asked the wounded man.

"I'm only scratched," said the Carcajou calmly. "But
f I had—Anne, throw me a gun and I'll show 'em—"

Anne Kendal, he saw, had snatched up a rifle and stood
n guard.

"Stop where you are!" she called to the trio.

"Look out, Roads," exclaimed Slade. "She's as sandy
s they make 'em, and she can shoot."

"Lady," said Bill Roads, "I've brought the law with
ne."

He showed her the badge inside the flap of his coat. The
trength for resistance wilted out of the erect body of the
;irl. Roads came striding up to her.

"It's straight law," he told her. "Don't you doubt me This bird goes back with me to look a jury in the eye that's where he goes. At last! Three years' work woun up!"

He dropped to one knee beside the Carcajou.

"Where did you get it?" he asked.

"Through the leg," said the Carcajou without emotion "It'll be all right in a few days. It didn't get the bone, I'n sure."

"Good for you," said Roads. "It was a long trail, Ban ner. But it was worth it! You don't mind if I fan you?"

He was searching the fallen man as he spoke.

"There's nothing else on me. Not even a penknife,' said the Carcajou.

"Are you trying to let him bleed to death?" exclaime Anne Kendal.

"Bleed to death?" said Roads happily. "I tell you, n one bullet could make a hole big enough to let out the lif of this hombre, lady. We'll tie him up, though."

He rolled up the trouser leg as he spoke and expose the wound, wonderfully small where the bullet had en tered, but with blood streaming from the back of the leg where the bullet had torn its way out of the flesh.

"Get some hot water. Some of that coffee would b better still," said Bill Roads. "We'll wash the blood awa and pack a bandage around it. I've got bandages in m shoulder pack. I never take Banner's trail without a first aid kit along. But it's last aid that I've been nearer needin a pile of times!"

He talked cheerfully in this manner as he went abou the bandaging of the wound, with the girl helping skill fully.

Horn and Slade were equally exultant for different rea sons. Horn had found the canvas sack in which the washe dust had been stored. He weighted the ponderous burden with his hand and shouted with glee.

"They been doing our work for us, Slade!" he cried. "We just been having a little vacation while they worked for us!"

"You fool," said Slade to the Carcajou, "did you think we wouldn't come back? But it was luck that ran us into Bill Roads, I got to admit. But we'd been back, anyway. It ain't the gold, only. It's your scalp we wanted mostly, you sneaking traitor."

Old Tom said: "If one of you is a policeman, which is it?"

He was standing, grasping his staff with both hands, leaning upon it, a favorite attitude of his, as though he were braced to receive a shock from any direction.

"I've got the warrant and all," answered Bill Roads. "You're Old Tom, I guess? You've got a reputation up here, Tom. How d'you come to be trying to beat Horn and Slade out of their mine?"

"Their mine?" exclaimed Old Tom. "Who said it was their mine?"

"He can lie, too, old and blind as he is; he can see his way to the telling of a pretty good lie!" said Slade. "Don't be wasting your time on the old fool, Roads!"

The bandaging finished, Roads stood up. He shrugged his shoulders.

"What do I care about the infernal mine!" he exclaimed. He pointed to the prostrate form of the Carcajou. "There's my gold mine, and my diamond mine, too!"

181

CHAPTER 16
Journey's End

"THAT'S RIGHT, ROADS, BUT YOU'RE GOING TO GET A slice out of this from us, too," said Slade. "You just herd the girl and the old man off along with the Carcajou. Just clean 'em off the claim for us, and—"

At that moment Anne Kendal spoke up: "He's honest, John. This man is honest, I think."

The Carcajou nodded. "Bill Roads is one of the honest men, I guess; or honest bloodhounds, for that matter. Call him whichever you please. He can shoot at a man from behind; that's his style."

"It was a bad play I made there in Steuermann's," admitted Roads. "I'm sorry about that, and I got what was coming to me for it. I went sort of crazy, I think, when I saw you at last, after the long hunt, Banner. Something went crash in my head. I wanted to see you dead; that was all!"

"You intend to take us away from the claim and then turn it over to Horn and Slade?" the girl said to Roads.

"That's what I intend to do," said Bill Roads. "They've helped me to turn the best trick—"

"Will you listen to our side of the story?"

"Hey, Bill, don't be a fool," said Charley Horn. "She's the slickest little liar that ever stepped in a shoe!"

Bill Roads frowned. "Down in Texas, we don't call any woman a liar. Go on, lady, and let's hear what you have to say."

It didn't take long. She told the entire story in a hundred words. But truth weighted every phrase that she uttered. She reached the death of Dinsmore, the attempts of Old Tom to locate his young partner, how those attempts had been blocked by the knavery of Horn. Then Bill Roads broke in, saying: "Horn, this sounds pretty straight and pretty black to me!"

"Look, Bill," said Charley Horn. "You ain't simple enough to believe what a girl says—this far north, are you?"

Laying a friendly hand on the shoulder of Bill Roads, he patted that shoulder familiarly and laughed a little. Therein he made a vital error, because the laughter had no ring of conviction in it. Bill Roads stepped back from under the caressing hand and shook his head.

"This here," he pronounced, "is no case I can settle out of hand. No, sir; it's gotta be done by course of law. You arrange it when you get back outside. Maybe the best thing is for the whole lot of you to come outside with me, and then the law'll say what's what. Old Tom, here, has a pretty good name. I've heard a hundred men talk about him, and never a slanderous word."

"Wait a minute, Bill," pleaded Slade; "you mean you're gonna make us waste our time? Is that what you mean? Make us mush all the way back to get the cursed law to—"

"Don't curse the law, brother," said Bill Roads, growing more and more cold. "Maybe you're all right, you two. But if Horn double-crossed a blind man, while another man was dying, then Horn oughta be burned alive, and maybe you alongside of him! That's what it looks like to me!''

While Roads was speaking to Slade, the latter gave one hard, bright look to Horn, and the latter stepped instantly behind the man of the law. Now, with a very faint and cruel smile pulling at the corners of his mouth, Slade raised a forefinger.

''Take it, you!'' gasped Horn, and crashed the butt end of his revolver against the skull of Bill Roads.

The man of the law made one stumbling step forward, stretching a hand toward the ground to save himself from the inevitable fall, with the other hand tugging at his revolver.

But blackness was in his brain and, as the revolver came forth, it fell to the ground, with its owner beside it. Not uselessly did it fall, however; for the Carcajou, giving his body a sudden pivotal movement, came up on his good knee and one hand, holding the Colt in his other hand.

It was a twin brother of the gun he himself had lost the moment before. There were no sights. They had been filed away like the trigger.

There would be only five shots in that gun; no one would have a cartridge under the hammer that was controlled by such a delicate spring as this which operated in the old-fashioned, single-action Colt.

To the grasp of the Carcajou, nothing could have been more welcome. Instantly it was scooped up. He was ready to shoot as Slade yelled: ''Behind you, Charley! For God's sake, the Carcajou!''

Slade's own gun was out. Charley Horn reversed the position of his revolver and spun toward the Carcajou, shooting as he turned. One bullet struck the ground and knocked a handful of turf into the face of the Carcajou. But the latter was not perturbed. Without haste and without delay, he fired.

Charley Horn promptly turned his back, raised his face

oward the sky, to which he seemed babbling a wordless omplaint. Then he fell on his back, dead.

Slade saw that bullet strike. He heard the dull, heavy, ounding stroke of it as it went home, at least. And the pirit went out of him. He had an idea what the Carcajou ould do with a gun. He had seen him shoot birds out of rees. And now the heart of Jimmy Slade fell. The big Colt in his own hand became a mere encumbrance. He ast it far from him. He screamed as he turned and fled, nd threw out his arms as if to grasp at safety.

The Carcajou raised his gun.

"No, no, John!" cried the girl.

He looked across at her. The evil went out of his heart, nd he dropped his hand; as Jimmy Slade disappeared into he brush.

They were left alone, suddenly, with the senseless body f Roads on the ground, and the groaning, curious voice f Old Tom murmuring: "What's happened? Somebody ell me! Anne, John, somebody tell me!"

But the Carcajou barely heard the question; what mat-ered was the shining eyes of the girl, as she answered: 'John has saved us all again. That's all. It's the same old tory, with one dead man added. I don't think Roads is adly hurt."

Roads, in fact, was on his feet in five minutes. For an-ther five he sat staring about him, before he spoke. "You ould have tagged me while I was down and out, Banner!" e remarked.

"It's all right, Roads," said John Banner. "They don't lay the old game that way up here, this far north."

"I'm gonna take a walk and think things over," mut-ered the man of the law.

He picked himself up and strode off into the under-rowth, his head bent forward, his whole attitude one of hought.

"He won't come back," said the girl, looking toward the Carcajou.

"He won't come back," said Old Tom. "That leaves a blind man, a wounded man, and a girl. Can we beat the game?"

"We can beat the game," said the Carcajou. "I'll be on my feet again in a couple of weeks."

"Ah, man!" muttered Old Tom. "How can we reward you?"

"There's only one reward I'm going to try for," said the Carcajou, staring.

Anne Kendal met the glance steadily, unabashed, unblushing, and she smiled her answer.

"Only," said the Carcajou, "I'd still need a lot of teaching, and a lot of remaking, and all I know is I want to learn. Slaughter and I can learn at the same time."

"You know, John," said the girl, "this far north the days are pretty long; we could learn a good deal together."

She stopped. A harsh, metallic calling came faintly to them out of the air and, looking up, the Carcajou saw a scattering wedge of wild geese flying toward the north. Let them go, he felt, for he, John Banner, had reached the end of all his journeying.

HISTORICAL NOVELS
OF THE AMERICAN FRONTIERS

<u>DON WRIGHT</u>

☐	58991-2	THE CAPTIVES	$4.50
☐	58992-0		Canada $5.50
☐	58989-0	THE WOODSMAN	$3.95
☐	58990-4		Canada $4.95

<u>DOUGLAS C. JONES</u>

☐	58459-7	THE BAREFOOT BRIGADE	$4.50
☐	58460-0		Canada $5.50
☐	58457-0	ELKHORN TAVERN	$4.50
☐	58458-9		Canada $5.50
☐	58453-8	GONE THE DREAMS AND DANCING	$3.95
		(Winner of the Golden Spur Award)	
☐	58454-6		Canada $4.95
☐	58450-3	SEASON OF YELLOW LEAF	$3.95
☐	58451-1		Canada $4.95

<u>EARL MURRAY</u>

☐	58596-8	HIGH FREEDOM	$4.95
☐	58597-6		Canada 5.95

Buy them at your local bookstore or use this handy coupon:
Clip and mail this page with your order.

Publishers Book and Audio Mailing Service
P.O. Box 120159, Staten Island, NY 10312-0004

Please send me the book(s) I have checked above. I am enclosing $_____
(please add $1.25 for the first book, and $.25 for each additional book to
cover postage and handling. Send check or money order only—no CODs.)

Name _____

Address _____

City _____ State/Zip _____

Please allow six weeks for delivery. Prices subject to change without notice.

MORE
HISTORICAL NOVELS
OF THE AMERICAN FRONTIERS

<u>JOHN BYRNE COOK</u>

THE SNOWBLIND MOON TRILOGY
(Winner of the Golden Spur Award)

☐	58150-4	BETWEEN THE WORLDS	$3.95
☐	58151-2		Canada $4.95
☐	58152-0	THE PIPE CARRIERS	$3.95
☐	58153-9		Canada $4.95
☐	58154-7	HOOP OF THE NATION	$3.95
☐	58155-5		Canada $4.95

<u>W. MICHAEL GEAR</u>

☐	58304-3	LONG RIDE HOME	$3.95
☐	58305-1		Canada $4.95

<u>JOHN A. SANDFORD</u>

☐	58843-6	SONG OF THE MEADOWLARK	$3.95
☐	58844-4		Canada $4.95

<u>JORY SHERMAN</u>

☐	58873-8	SONG OF THE CHEYENNE	$2.95
☐	58874-6		Canada $3.95
☐	58871-1	WINTER OF THE WOLF	$3.95
☐	58872-X		Canada $4.95

Buy them at your local bookstore or use this handy coupon:
Clip and mail this page with your order.

Publishers Book and Audio Mailing Service
P.O. Box 120159, Staten Island, NY 10312-0004

Please send me the book(s) I have checked above. I am enclosing $_____
(please add $1.25 for the first book, and $.25 for each additional book to
cover postage and handling. Send check or money order only — no CODs.)

Name _____

Address _____

City _____ State/Zip _____

Please allow six weeks for delivery. Prices subject to change without notice.